SHERLOCK HOLMES AND

THE MENACING MOORS

a tribute to Holmes and Watson and the mystique of the mysterious Moors.

Allan Mitchell

D0880210

Paperback ISBN 978-1-78092-746-6
ePub ISBN 978-1-78092-747-3
PDF ISBN 978-1-78092-748-0

Published in the UK by MX Publishing
335 Princess Park Manor, Royal Drive,
London, N11 3GX www.mxpublishing.co.uk
Cover design by www.staunch.com

Introduction

Sherlock Holmes is of a place in time, later-Victorian London in fact, a place in time captivating and intriguing but tantalisingly just out of reach, though holding our minds in a hazy cloud of memories which are not our own but which we have constructed from the writings of the times into which we have been immersed and in which we feel we have taken part.

Sherlock is the one with "other knowledge", knowledge which we and Sherlock share, and no other, except for the snippets which Doctor Watson is permitted for his stories. We feel for Sherlock when credit for his efforts go to an undeserving Lestrade or Gregson. His mood swings infuriate us and his interest in the cocaine bottle is cause for concern but we begrudgingly understand that his exceptional mind craves stimulation and exercise. He is the flawed genius and there is a basic goodness about him, and he has a simple sense of justice – punishment for the unrepentant villain, compassion for the helpless victim.

For so many of us, Sherlock Holmes exists on the platform of a smoky railway station, at the telegraph office writing out an urgent communication to Lestrade, in his Baker Street rooms jumping from his chair to greet a young lady who has travelled by dog cart and train to engage his services, on the Thames in a steam launch trying to catch the villain making off with ill-gotten jewels, out on the moors in pursuit of a large incandescent dog and a butterfly-hunting fiend, and doing whatever our minds can conjure up from the adventures we have shared with Holmes and Watson and those other characters born of the mind and experiences of Arthur Conan Doyle.

Sherlock: we find his image emerging from those oldish-style black and white illustrations prepared by Sidney Paget for The Stand; the locations of his exploits are mysterious and intriguing; his opponents are evil; and, despite the fact that his magnificent pipe was a later invention by others maintaining and expanding the world of Sherlock, he does has a great hat!

So many times has Sherlock tried to fade away to become a vague and distant memory; so many times have we dragged him from his hiding place on that dingy, dark, smoke-ridden Victorian street to take us on just one more adventure, in his time, or in ours. While our minds can do that, Sherlock Holmes can never die. Sir Arthur Conan Doyle couldn't kill him off, so what chance us?

Sherlock is as real as we want him to be, as real as Robin Hood, as real as their arch-rivals, Moriarty and the Sheriff of Nottingham – his character exists in our minds, in many ways like another two-dimensional black and white character from a later era, now distant and ever-retreating, one Winston Churchill. Sherlock and Winston can still be found around London, embodied in its fabric - statues to both exist, museums celebrate the life and achievements of both. However, while one can visit the tomb of the famous wartime leader, Sherlock has no need of one.

CONTENTS

THE MENACING MOORS

THE SUMMONS

Long overshadowed by more recent and pressing cases requiring the remarkable cerebral capabilities of Mister Sherlock Holmes, the details surrounding the case of the mysterious Moors of Devon, the looming battlements of Baskerville Hall and the devilish howl of the Hound of Hell had been stored away in the Sleuth's brain-attic, filed and catalogued for retrieval if ever the need arose for their consultation.

The morning sun of Autumn had yet to rise and herald the start of yet another overcast and gloomy day, but Holmes, being so often the case, was already awake. Not yet dressed for the day, he was surprised to hear Mrs Hudson's knuckles rapping on his door and calling out, "Mister Holmes, it's an urgent message I have – just delivered by special messenger." Opening his door, he saw a sleepily dishevelled Mrs Hudson holding a letter in her outstretched hand. Taking the letter and examining both sides of its envelope, Holmes said briskly, "Thank you, Mrs Hudson - what could be so urgent to warrant my attention at this unearthly hour?" Mrs Hudson, yawning and far less than interested, replied, "A good detective would look inside the envelope before asking me silly questions. It's back to bed for me – it's far too early for breakfast!" Holmes, recovering his composure, addressed his landlady more gently, saying, "Indeed, Mrs Hudson, but I fear I'll be in need of a pot of strong, hot coffee to stir my brain if someone is summoning me so urgently."

Further examining the envelope's exterior and noting the erratic manner of the handwriting and the lack of crumpling or folding of the letter, and the absence of a postage stamp, features which spoke, firstly, of its urgency and, then, of its carriage in a despatch satchel by a special courier, Holmes reached for his letter-opening stiletto, a souvenir of a vendetta case he had handled in Palermo some years earlier, slipped its blade under the sealed fold of the envelope and, in one rapid movement, sliced it open to reveal the contents. As was his habit, Holmes examined those contents before retrieving a single folded sheet of paper. Unfolding this, Holmes adjusted the gas lamp to its maximum brightness, sat and read, on both sides, what emerged as a desperate plea for help. Jumping to his feet, he ran to Watson's room, banged on its door and shouted.....

"The game is afoot, Watson! Pull on your boots!
Grab your hat and your coat and bring something that shoots
For we're after a foe who has nothing to lose -
Your old Army revolver is what I would choose."

"You should check it for bullets - you'll need a full six
But you may need some more if we get in a fix;
So bring a whole packet – it might come in handy –
And do not forget that half bottle of brandy."

"And that lantern we used in our Whitechapel caper,
Of which you have written for some London paper,
I have filled it with oil and trimmed up its wick
So, the fog, we'll now see through, no matter how thick."

"Between you and your gun and your military bluster
And me with my cudgel and old knuckleduster
And us both with some steady reliable light,
I think we'll be fine if it comes to a fight."

"For we're off to the Moors where the wind blows and howls
And where, after each sundown, an evil thing prowls

Seeking souls for some vile and insidious rite -
It's a beast full of fury, spilling over with spite."

"We must both keep our wits and not once drop our guard
Or the lesson we'll learn will be ever so hard.
Courage, John Watson, we'll need all we've got
If we are, by this demon, once put on the spot."

"And such agents of Evil are not known to rest
So it's crucial that each of us strive to his best
To reach down to the depths of his soul and extract
Every smidgin of nerve that a man can exact."

Watson woke with a start at the noise Sherlock made
And he knew he was in for some new escapade.
"Holmes, is that you? What was that about Moors?
It's really too cold to go roaming outdoors."

Sherlock made no reply, but sat scanning his map
Of the wastelands of Dartmoor laid out on his lap;
He looked up with a face full of anguish and gloom
As a bleary-eyed Watson emerged from his room.

Watson's eyes were half open, his hair was a mess
As he said to Holmes gruffly, *"My Stars! I confess*
That my slumber's been ruined; my rest's at an end;
That wasn't the way to arouse a good friend."

"I was dreaming, you know, of a field, green and warm,
And a trickling brook and a miniature swarm
Of those midges which gather and hover above
Any moisture they find in this land that I love."

"I was watching the swans sailing by in their fleets
And reflections of clouds forming little white sheets

6

In a blue English sky when, alas, my delight
Was destroyed when I woke with a terrible fright."

"There was nothing but darkness where once a bright sun
Had been filling my dreams full of sunbeams and fun.
What has happened to drag me from slumber so deep?
Is there some drastic reason you won't let me sleep?"

Holmes held up the letter – a message delivered
Just minutes before and at which he had shivered
When reading its contents – his blood had gone cold -
The words which he read hinted horrors untold.

"Mister Holmes," it had started, *"there's no time to waste -*
Please drop what you are doing and come with great haste -
We need you – we're facing a beast that's not mortal -
To the horrors of Hell, Satan's opened a portal."

"We remember the time when you came to assist
Young Sir Henry from horrors which came through the mist
In the form of a hound which was painted to glow
And to hunt down its quarry and, death, then bestow."

"We had thought it a hound which was sent straight from Hell
As the Baskerville legend, for centuries, would tell
Of the pact made with Satan in times long ago
By Sir Henry's ancestor, that fiendish Hugo."

"The hound we all saw, we believed, had been sent
From the Devil himself through some Satanic vent;
But you, Mister Holmes, were the one who dispelled
All such fears, and who had all such notions repelled."

"But now something new and more sinister's come
To the Moors, a foul thing which has caused more than some

To believe that, this time, it's pure evil they face -
Dartmoor, Mister Holmes, is a Satanic place."

"There have been fearful screams from the Moor in the night
When its creatures succumbed to a terrible plight;
There've been ponies dismembered and sheep torn to bits
And one hardy old shepherd was found taking fits."

"And that shepherd has sworn that, a form, he had seen
In the shadowy twilight as it passed between
All its victims, while killing and maiming all those
In its path – though, a few, it deliberately chose."

"What this demon might be and what form it might take
Is not easy to say, but there are some who'd make
The assumption that it gets some demonic thrill
From the roars they have heard it make after a kill."

"It's a fact", it continued, *"that, unlike that Hound*
You encountered before, this thing utters a sound
Which would frighten that canine right out of its fur
And would send the thing off like a snivelling cur."

"All the hamlets and farms settled deep in the Moors,
Have been once again called on to bar all their doors
And to shutter their windows, from dusk until dawn,
To what some folks are calling the Devil's own spawn."

"The Police cannot help us, the Army won't come;
So we're hopeful you're able to render us some
Form of help in this crisis - we need steady hands
And strong minds for whatever this evil demands."

"We await your response to our earnest appeal -
Your help and assistance would mean a great deal.

Here, the people are frightened right down to their bones.
Can you help us? Yours hopefully, Timothy Jones."

"Watson – do you recall from our Baskerville case,
It was Timothy Jones who had offered to chase
Down whatever had killed his landlord and his friend?
His offer was not taken up, in the end."

"Recall him, I do, and remember his strength."
Replied Watson, *"Also, that he's travelled the length*
And the breadth of those Moors – he knows better than most
How to stick to his guns and to stand at his post."

"He's ex-Army, you know – an Artillery man,
And, if he says there's danger, it's certain we can
Take his word on the matter – the man is quite sound;
In the Crimean conflict, the man stood his ground."

"That was some time ago, but I hear what you say."
Holmes responded, *"The man was quite brave in his day."*
"He remains so today," added Watson, *"though older,"*
"And he is of the type who'd be no less the bolder."

"Holmes, we must act, and we must do it now.
I don't know what has happened but, clearly, somehow
We must render assistance." said Watson, appalled,
"Our friend requests help - we should answer when called."

"Give me ten minutes, Sherlock, and I will be ready -
My valise is half packed and my gun hand is steady;
But I must confess, Holmes, talk of Satanic portals
Is testing my nerve – I'd prefer to fight mortals."

"Mister Timothy Jones, I recall now, was not
Of the type to lose nerve when confronting a lot

Of hearsay, superstitious. " said Holmes, in reply,
"There's a fiend behind this - we must find who, and why."

"First things first - and, so, Watson, we must clear the head.
Now, I think that I hear Mrs Hudson's soft tread
So please open the door for that lady, sincere,
For, if I'm not mistaken, our coffee is here."

Mrs Hudson appeared with two cups and a pot
Full of coffee, quite strong, black and steaming and hot;
"I have bread and cold meat," she said, *"eat on the way -*
For I fear you're off into a miserable day."

"Mrs Hudson, You Angel!" said Sherlock, elated,
"The needs of our work you have anticipated.
I, myself, can eat little then be on my way,
But Watson needs sustenance throughout the day."

Doctor Watson said, *"Holmes, I'm a medical man*
And, to go on a fast, if it's needed, I can.
But to maintain good health and to be at my peak,
I must eat sensibly - otherwise I go weak."

"Then eat all you can hold, and then carry the rest,
For we'll both need to be at our absolute best.
But we'll rest on the train and have meals when we stop,"
Replied Sherlock, "assuming we get time to shop."

Then, into his satchel, essentials, Holmes threw,
While Watson got ready, then stopped while he drew
Out his pistol and bullets from where they had lain,
Cleaned and oiled and ready, till needed again.

Mrs Hudson, meanwhile, had stepped out from her hall
And down onto the street with her whistle to call

10

For a cab which she knew would be waiting nearby
And, when she heard it coming, she gave out a cry.

"Mister Holmes, Doctor Watson, you've no time to waste;
If you'd make that first train you must come in great haste
For your Hansom is coming, it's just up the street.
Get moving, the both of you – don't drag your feet."

A quick telegraph message, to Jones, Sherlock wrote
To be sent without fail to reach the remote
Dartmoor residents quickly to help quell their fears -
Jones must know that his plea did not fall on deaf ears.

Mrs Hudson said she, as she had done before,
Would make certain the message was sent, and she swore
That it would be despatched to be sent to the Moors
Once the Telegraph Office had opened its doors.

Holmes and Watson rushed out and were soon under way
In that Hansom to catch the first train of the day;
The cabbie was shouting, the horse's hooves clacked
As it galloped away as the whip whooshed and cracked.

When they got to the station, Holmes gave out a shout,
Threw a coin to the cabbie as he scrambled out
Of the Hansom, while Watson was close on his tail
For the engineer's whistle had started to wail.

Two tickets, Holmes bought as the engineer's hand
Pressed down hard on the throttle to make his demand
On the engine for movement – a little to start,
And then more and more – it was time to depart.

And departing, it was, as our pair saw the train
Start to move, just a little, when put under strain;

So they sprinted to catch it while carriages moaned
As the engine pulled at them and shuddered and groaned.

A door opened wide as Holmes pulled at its latch;
Watson jumped in the carriage they'd raced hard to catch
And was followed by Holmes and the door was slammed shut
And they both knew how closely their time had been cut.

"A close thing, that, Watson, but make it, we did."
Said Holmes as he stretched and then gingerly slid
His valise to the luggage rack high on the wall
Although Watson threw his as he wasn't so tall.

Then, as Holmes settled down in his seat, his great mind
Lost all thoughts of the rush as it turned to the kind
Which considered the problems his clients might face
And was glad when he felt the train gathering pace.

"Before dawn, we now start for the menacing Moors;
Before dusk, we must get ourselves safely indoors."
Uttered Sherlock who knew there was danger, extreme,
If the folks of the Moors spoke of evil, supreme.

Holmes considered the case as strange paradox
In complete isolation inside a strange box
Set on wheels for relocating both Watson and him
To where-ever they'd like on some magical whim.

Holmes' strange box wasn't magic, but it gave him time
To consider the points of what could be a crime;
He'd go over the note, give each section its due,
For within every line, there might nestle a clue.

But the single sole clue that the Sleuth could discern
Was of terror, extreme – this was cause for concern.

Were there gains to be made? Were there fortunes to win?
These were questions Holmes pondered with utter chagrin.

THE MOORS

As Holmes pondered his problems, he reached for his pipe
Nestled in his coat pocket – he wanted to wipe
Away every distraction - diversions, despatch;
But he'd pay his respects before striking a match.

To Sherlock, his pipe was a friend, old and true;
And, as such, when consulted, was given its due
In respect and regard as tradition demanded -
A pipe must be coaxed – it could not be commanded.

With two fingers and thumb of his left hand, he'd grip
His old pipe at the base of its bowl and then slip
The same fingers and thumb of his right in his pouch
Of tobacco of brand of which Sherlock could vouch.

Holmes would then hold his pipe out in line with his face
And would take a few moments in which he might trace
Any stains on its bowl, any scratch on its stem,
Any vestige of cases which passed between them.

Then, with ritual fervour, he'd pull out the plug
Of tobacco and pack it until it was snug
In the bowl of his pipe and, then, up to his lips
Raise the pipe until mouthpiece and teeth came to grips.

With two hands now unhindered, he'd reach to withdraw,
From the slide of its box, any match without flaw
And would strike on the box, with this Lucifer's head,
The friction pad, or on his boot sole, instead.

In one spluttering second, it would burst into fire -
Holmes would lift up his hand so that he could admire
This force, elemental, he had in his power -
A force of the gods which might cause men to cower.

With such actions and thoughts, to his old friend, he'd pay
Great respect and, in doing so, thus pave the way
To ignite the tobacco – to set it afire,
Take a draught, long and deep; to his thoughts, then retire.

Sherlock thought of the Moors and considered the hold
Which they held on the mind, and of legends so old
That their meanings were lost, though the mystery remained,
And from thinking out loud, he would not be restrained.

"It gets cold on those wastes where this deviltry flies
And wind carries the sound of bloodcurdling cries
Of a victim in terror, its violent death -
The snarls of the killer, the victim's last breath."

"Where the sun has departed the wintery sky
And the clouds summon evil as they fly on by
As they fracture and filter the moon's feeble light,
And an agent, malignant, steps into the night."

"And, to many a traveller, these Moors have spelled doom;
And a poor wayward soul disappears in the gloom
Never more to return, never more to be seen
In this world or the next –somewhere, lost, in-between."

"The expanses of Dartmoor, Watson, are the kind
Which contrive to play tricks on the unwary mind;
When the sunlight is dimmed and the fog has rolled in,
The eyes are deceived and the head starts to spin."

"There are no points of reference, the senses are fooled
And the present and past are collectively pooled;
It's an easy thing, Watson, to lose in that place,
One's mind and one's bearings, in time and in space."

"One need only consider the Baskerville hound
And the fear such a legend could cause with the sound
Of a large baying dog, not to mention the paint -
When it glowed in the dark, sturdy fellows went faint."

"Just remember the fear and the panic which grew
In our minds and our stomachs, although we both knew
That the hound we saw glowing was not sent from Hell
But from someone whose murderous greed we would quell."

"Such fears are within us from when we are born
And are so deeply set that they cannot be torn
From the darkest recesses of rational brains
So we lock them in dungeons and keep them in chains."

"But, although they're in chains, we at times hear them rattle
As our primeval fears try to break free and battle
Our most rational thoughts – so, alert, we must stay
And, from giving fears freedom, we must steer away."

"There are other tales, Watson, and some are so old
That nobody knows how they began, but they're told
By the families of Dartmoor, year in and year out,
And, every so-often, a new one will sprout."

"Just two hundred and fifty short years have elapsed
Since folks from Widecombe-on-the-Moor had collapsed
In convulsions, one night, in a great thunderstorm,
Upon seeing Satan take on physical form."

"Although, since those times, many notions we've shaken,
It seems, even now, superstitions are taken
Quite seriously by those deep in the Moor -
Our appreciation of this fact is quite poor."

"There's an old Roman fort, so the locals would tell,
Set atop Hunters' Tor and where lost soldiers dwell
In a darkness, eternal, except for one night
In each month as they march under Luna's full light."

"Many people swear blind they have seen such a sight
As the Moor comes alive in that eerie moonlight
And the dead form their ranks and march forth from the fort,
Perhaps, overdue comrades, to find and support."

"And the ancient stone circles are said to have been
Formed on one Sabbath's night as some dancers were seen
To have danced 'round in rings and were turned into stone
For, to dance on the Sabbath, God would not condone."

"Though we know that these circles of stone are far older
Than recorded history, it takes someone bolder
Than I to declare such beliefs incorrect -
Such notions, the folks on the Moor, would reject."

"Lady Howard killed husbands, too many, so she
Every night, as a black dog, is now forced to flee
Running fast at the side of a coach made from bone
Struck from each murdered husband, till she can atone."

"Such legends are needed so districts, remote,
Can have folklore, distinct, which their people can quote
And retell as their own – for these stories will bond
These communities when there's a need to respond."

"Old Dewer, the Devil, deep within Wishtman Wood,
Once would frighten a traveller right where he stood;
Dewer's hounds would then harry him, gasping for breath,
To the Dewerstone Tor where he'd fall to his death."

"These Moors," added Holmes, *"have such stories to tell*
Upon which no sane person should ever long dwell.
But I must clear my mind of what people might say
And examine the facts in my own unique way."

Sherlock sat in his seat and observed a dim glow
As the sun, still unseen, was attempting to show
It was time for the night to give way to the day,
And he'd need as much daylight as might come his way.

For the hours of daylight were shortening fast
As the seasons had changed and the sunshine would last
For too few dismal hours – it was vital they get
To the Moors and indoors well before the sun set.

Sherlock puffed on his pipe he held ever so dear
With such vigour that, from his great mind, he could clear
All invalid deductions it made prematurely -
The facts in this case would emerge, though obscurely.

Watson munched on the bread he had stuffed in a sack
And he offered friend Sherlock a share as a snack;
But our Sleuth, although grateful, politely refused,
And then Watson spoke up, just a little bemused.

"Do you have any thoughts on what evil might lurk
On the Moors, and what danger exists in the murk
And the gloom which could terrify sturdy folk so?
Can whatever it is be destroyed or made go?"

"It's too early to tell, and conjecture is wrong
If we don't have the facts." answered Holmes, thinking long
And quite hard on the matter, while puffing away
On his pipe while refusing to yield to dismay.

But, alas, Watson's mind was alive with the thought
That, well, it might be a foul demon which sought
To take hold of the living and take them to Hell
And there, with old Satan, forever to dwell.

For, unlike his friend Holmes, Doctor Watson could not
Put up walls in his mind, walls constructed to blot
Out superfluous data; his mind wasn't able
To separate fact from a primeval fable.

Sherlock had his beliefs, but his prayer was the life
Which he led when out fighting the crime which was rife
In that great cesspool, London, the country and town;
Providence, up on-high, though, would not let him down.

Watson was of the type which held Scripture supreme;
He'd been raised on a fearful Old Testament theme;
Deep down in his mind lurked each demon and imp
Which he feared from his childhood and still sent him limp.

Just the hint of a spectre would send a cold shiver
Right throughout his body and cause him to quiver
Until he could set things to rights in his mind;
When it came to such things, Watson's reason was blind.

But the train chugged along at a comfortable pace
Causing Watson to doze and to go to that place
He'd inhabited just before Sherlock barged in
And had broken his slumber and dreams with his din.

He would open an eye and look out at the scene
For a few fleeting moments, then seek the serene
Little world of his dreams of his own native land,
While Holmes was transfixed by the problem at hand.

The train steamed on west through a country-side bleak
While Watson dreamed on with the land at the peak
Of its glory, in Summer and sunshine galore -
He did not want to dwell on what might be in store.

Sherlock said nothing more for the rest of the trip -
Not a point of conjecture, not even a quip
On the nature of crime and the criminal class;
His gaze was transfixed, his eyes seemed of glass.

At Exeter station, the day was half done
But they had to wait further, till twenty-to-one,
For the train which would take them to Jones and the brute
Which was bringing such horror to folks, resolute.

"If this train leaves on time and it keeps up its speed,
We will have all the time that we're surely to need
To get out to the village and safely inside
Where we and the rest, on a plan, can decide."

The train did leave on time and it kept up its speed
And, so, Watson and Holmes, were convinced they, indeed,
Would arrive in good time to be out on the scent
Of the beast, assuming their message was sent.

But soon the train slowed to a pitiful rate
And it seemed there would be a perpetual spate
Of delays, and of stops where no one would appear,
But the train was on time and their station was near.

The station was small and was almost deserted
But Timothy Jones had been duly alerted
By telegram and, so, had travelled to meet
Holmes and Watson through rain and a great deal of sleet.

He had travelled an hour and waited one more
With the barest of shelter to shield him before
He could hear, in the distance, the sound of the train
Puffing hard up the grade, belching smoke under strain.

He stepped onto the platform, umbrella in hand
And two waterproof coats of the Macintosh brand;
The engine's hard puffing had started to slow,
His hopes in the form of the Great Sleuth in tow.

He had food for the travellers, some brandy to sip,
For he knew they would need sustenance for the trip
And some internal fire to keep out the cold -
When one's out on the Moor, local knowledge is gold.

In the bone-jarring carriage, Holmes dozed as he could
But stayed largely awake with the hope that he would
See his way through the puzzle before he'd arrive
If only, this leg of his trip, he'd survive.

Next to Sherlock, sprawled over a bench seat obliquely,
The old trooper, Watson, was, somewhat uniquely,
Maintaining his sleep, when the ear-splitting scream
Of the train whistle spoiled a new idyllic dream.

"It's a shame that steam whistle would not let me sleep."
Complained Watson on waking, *"I do like a deep
And sustained form of slumber. I did hear that call
And I fear, for some time, I'll have no sleep at all."*

Sherlock, though not sleeping, might have been in a trance
But arose and said, *"Watson, it's time to advance*
To the battleground, Man - we'll sleep when we're dead
But, as we're both alive, we'll seek action instead."

Jones had signalled the driver he needed to stop
For as long as it took his two charges to hop
To a platform swept madly by wind-blown rain -
Both wished, at that moment, they'd stayed in the train.

The umbrella was useless – two coats were confessed
To be items, essential, perhaps even blessed,
For they covered their contents from head down to heel,
And with sou'wester hats, no raindrops would they feel.

Watson's peaked cap was soaked and was dripping away,
Sherlock's deerstalker sodden and useless that day;
They felt quite unprepared though, on Dartmoor, they'd been
Some years back, though its worst, clearly, they hadn't seen.

Before one word was spoken, the Macintosh coats
Were each thrown on in haste and, as snug as two stoats,
Holmes and Watson were greeted by Jones' refrain:
"I'm afraid that there's no getting out of this rain."

"But the wagon is here; I have ample food handy
And you should help yourselves to that bottle of brandy;
Pull that tarpaulin over your heads and sit back -
Get what comfort you can - it's a bumpy old track."

"For the wagon, I'm sorry; the coach was away
And it wouldn't be back till much later today.
We've just over an hour of daylight remaining
And I wouldn't blame either of you for complaining."

Watson countered to Jones, *"We're both fed and quite dry*
And we're here to do battle – and it would be a wry
Sort of soldier who'd dither because of some rain -
Our comrade has called us – we shall not complain."

"Well said," agreed Sherlock, *"so, Jones, lead us on*
To where-ever it is that the evil demon
Or whatever it is has been causing you trouble.
Can you get both your horses to trot at the double?"

"Mister Holmes, we must go at a good steady pace
For it is a poor track, and a wet one, we trace
Through these Moors; and I fear that a spill
Would provide that foul demon with one easy kill."

"Or should I say three?" Jones continued to say,
"For the beast might kill all that it finds in its way."
"Then, steady, it is." Holmes, corrected, agreed,
"We'll continue at what's an appropriate speed."

For the first times in weeks, Jones had managed a grin
At the dry gallows humour he'd shared with those in
His uncomfortable wagon – things were looking bright;
But he must press on now or he'd run out of light.

This last leg of their journey took just on an hour
Through a landscape rainswept and exceedingly dour,
Especially to Watson, for Holmes was detached -
The Moors offered beauty and terror, unmatched.

They arrived at the village, the sun setting low
On the western horizon, its faint reddish glow
Pushing hard through the cloud and, as though as a tease,
Now that they'd arrived, the rain started to ease.

"Get you in near the fire," said Timothy Jones
"You're probably frozen right down to your bones.
But as soon as you're warm, we will have you both fed
And I'll chance, from your trip, you'll be glad of a bed."

"I must unhitch the horses and get them inside
The old stables and fed – for, you see, they're my pride
And my joy and my friends – I live here on my own
As a widower man – to this life, I have grown."

"For my wife has been gone for these last twenty years
But, still, I look for her – I've shed many tears
For her memory. Forgive me, for often I've found
Myself talking as though she was here, still around."

"A good man, and true," whispered Watson, impressed
By the tenderness shown by their host. He repressed
The strong urge to reply to this man, brave and good -
A smile and a nod said that he understood.

The pair hung up their coats, placed their boots near the fire,
Moved as close to the mantle as they could desire;
They'd absorb as much heat as the flames could deliver -
It was warm in the house, but their bones made them shiver.

Some minutes would pass until Jones returned back
With an arm full of wood which he dropped on the stack
Of dry fuel for the fire: *"With these and the peat,*
We shall make the flames roar till we sweat from the heat."

"Come, gentlemen, sit, just as soon as you're able
To move from the fire, at our humble old table;
We've soup heating up on the stove and corned meat,
As much bread as you please and some cake for a treat."

"We will have the tea brewing, directly, but should
You desire something stronger, we certainly could
Find a flask of fine whiskey or, if you prefer,
We have rum in the pantry – I buy it for her."

With this last little quip and a knowing wry smile,
Jones had opened his home and his heart without guile;
Then he added, with laughter, *"I'll tell you no fibs -*
In the morning, it's porridge – it sticks to your ribs."

"And, as you've had a ride on my rickety cart,
You'll know what I mean by ribs coming apart.
When you're out on the Moors and you're this cold and wet -
You need all the internal glue you can get."

"Well, such things are important, but when you are done
With your meal, we shall speak of the thing, or the one,
Who's behind all our troubles, the blight on the land,
And if it is the work of some devilish hand."

"Indeed!" expressed Sherlock, *"That is why we have come*
To the Moors – to see if we can both be of some
Form of practical use in the problem you face
And to see, if a way to its source, we can trace."

"You have outlined the facts in the note that you sent
And, throughout our journey, my time has been spent
Mulling over your statements, expressions of fear,
But, what might be behind them, you haven't made clear."

"That is true," replied Jones in a hesitant tone,
"I recounted the rumours, but I'm all alone
In my thinking that somebody's behind what has come.
I know, Satan, it isn't - it's clearly someone."

THE OUTRAGE

When sufficiently warmed, Holmes and Watson both sat
At the table and consumed such a quantity that
Jones just had to laugh: *"Well, the Moors have a way
Of increasing the appetite amply, I'd say."*

*"Eat your fill, there is plenty - no need to hold back -
But I hope you're not squeamish – the facts are quite black.
I will tell you what's happened though, why, I can't say -
Stock wasn't just killed, it was put on display"*

*"I had mentioned, of course, that some Moor ponies died
In a horrible way – they were quite terrified
Of whatever attacked them – it must have been huge -
They had nowhere to run, not the barest refuge."*

*"Some limbs were torn out; some were bitten clean off
By some monstrous thing and, before you might scoff,
What remained of their bodies was neatly arranged
By something quite evil and surely deranged."*

*"Near the torsos, the heads were positioned correctly,
Although they'd been severed, and also, directly
Below the poor creature, four legs would project,
All pointing downward in their proper aspect."*

*"But the sheep, Mister Holmes, they were turned inside out,
More or less, with their heads and limbs scattered about
Though with heads to the south and with limbs to the north.
Mister Holmes, just what has, in these Moors, sallied forth?"*

*"But their insides were gone, Mister Holmes, that's a fact
And there wasn't a single one slightly intact.*

In a war, I have seen mangled horses galore
But no one ever put them together before."

"I had fears, I admit, of the Devil being here
On these Moors, cold and bleak and extremely austere;
But as soon as that letter, to you, was sent off,
I relaxed and, at such fears, absurd, had to scoff."

"And some people were missing, although that is not
So unusual around here, for many have got
To maintain all their fences, to clear out their drains,
For the damage is great with these hammering rains."

"There is one man, however, whose lengthy absence
Is of cause for concern, and we were to commence
A wide search on the Moor, as the weather permits,
Where Old Will Abernathy has pastures and pits."

"For we've not seen Old Will for a week and a day
And it's not like the man to get lost on his way
Through the Moors – it's a death trap, that's definite, but
Old Will could pass through it with both his eyes shut."

"Old Will knows all the trails and all of the bogs
And, besides, he took with him his very best dogs;
They both know their way through, even better than Will,
And they'd both come home barking if Will took a spill."

"There it is, Mister Holmes; it's a mystery indeed;
Let us hope it's not something whose secrets exceed
Even your esteemed powers; for if that is the case,
We might all be the victims of something quite base."

Before Holmes could reply, someone burst through the door
And fell heavily onto the bare timber floor;

"Come quickly, come quickly," in, Sam Worthy butted,
"They've found poor Old Will and they say he's been gutted."

The group rushed to the house of Old Will Abernathy
Where they met with its owner's distraught daughter Kathy;
Her sobs were distressing; her hands were hard clenched
And they both held the hanks of her hair she had wrenched.

Her state was quite wretched, she was in great distress;
She was ripping great patches of cloth from her dress;
She was close to hysterics, she spoke in a panic,
For the sight of her father had sent her quite manic.

"Miss Kathy, I've heard – it's a terrible thing
Which has happened this night. But I said I would bring
Mister Holmes and his friend, Doctor Watson, who would
Help us out with our problems, if anyone could."

"Mister Holmes, Doctor Watson, I'm so glad you've come."
Said the poor wretched woman, *"We surely need some*
Expert help, and, though all of your skills we admire,
I fear it's an exorcist that we require."

Old Will's body was found in his shed by his daughter
Who almost went mad at the sight of his slaughter;
She ran straight to a neighbour in utter distress -
It was all she could do, maddened screams, to suppress.

"I don't know, Mister Holmes, what my father has done
To deserve such a fate – he's not hurt anyone
In his life. He'd be gone for two days, perhaps three,
And then said, after that, we would have a week free."

"Now, my poor wretched father lies there, cold and dead,
But what had been done fills my mind with great dread;

His soul has been taken, his body defiled,
By some base wicked agent, depraved and reviled."

"Every bone in my father's poor body is broken -
His flesh has been savaged by something unspoken;
There are slashes and gashes and worse still, by far,
There's carved into his forehead, a five pointed star."

"That's a pentacle, surely, the Devil's own mark
Put there by an agent, demonic and stark;
What monster could do this? What's come to the Moors
To defile my poor father who ventured outdoors?"

Sherlock took Kathy's hand and said, *"Courage, My Dear.*
We must all keep our heads till the facts become clear.
Your father's a victim of some evil plot
And its agent is real – a spirit, it's not."

The group walked to Will's shed, but left Kathy behind
With a friend – they had fears for the state of her mind;
Sherlock asked all to wait so that he could inspect
Old Will's body for clues which were left to detect.

Sherlock looked at poor Will, but all pity had gone
From the face of the Sleuth, and his eyes fairly shone
As they scanned all Will's features, his wounds and the sign
Of great evil carved deep by an agent, malign.

Through his lens, he examined each tear and each scrape;
Noted eyes frozen open, a mouth, wide, agape;
With a ruler, he measured in inches, minute,
The distance 'tween scratches, his senses acute.

"His death was quite sudden –I feel that will be proved."
Sherlock said, though his eyes, from Old Will, hadn't moved;

"The wounds on his body, the marks on his face,
Have been made after death–all the signs I can trace."

"Come Watson," Holmes called to his medical friend,
"Tell us just what your medical eyes comprehend
Of this poor wretched victim, once healthy and hale.
Reconstruct, if you will, his injurious tale."

With emotions repressed, Watson studied Old Will
While the rest looked on fearfully, quiet and still;
Doctor Watson said dolefully, after a spell,
"In a war, I'd suspect an artillery shell."

"I recall, from the battles in Afghanistan,
Just what such a projectile can do to a man;
The force of the blast and the fragments of shell
Leave strongest of men like some reject from Hell."

"Well, of course, in this case, that's nonsensical thought;
But the wounds that I see tell me what should be sought
Is an agent of strength, superhuman, at least;
We must look for, I fear, an abominable beast."

"But what sort of a beast, on these Moors, could there be
That could crush a man's body so fully that he
Would retain not a bone which was fully intact?
Are we up against evil, incarnate, in fact?"

"Is it true, what the folks of the village fear most?
Are we up against some diabolical ghost?
Do we witness the coming of Satan's allies
And return of Beelzebub, Lord of the Flies."

Watson shuddered, near panicking, at such a thought,
And, against all his fears, the Professional fought

To retain his composure, his duty, observe;
In the view of the Public, he must keep his nerve.

"I'm a man honed on Science, superstition is just
The recourse of the ignorant, and so, I must
Keep my fears in control, be objective, and stay
Fully focussed and keep my emotions at bay."

He returned to Old Will, for he owed him the time
To determine if death was by mishap or crime;
He checked over Will's body and, after a lull,
He said, *"Holmes, there's a hole in the back of his skull."*

"It's a bullet hole, Holmes, of a calibre, small.
It would seem that our demon's a man, after all,
For I don't think a ghost would have need of a gun -
It would scare us to death for some devilish fun."

"Old Will's body is broken - violated, in fact -
And there isn't one part of him fully intact.
But the wounds that I see, as you rightly depicted,
Show signs of Will's death before they were inflicted."

"We should cover poor Will - it's a quite dreadful sight,"
Uttered Timothy Jones, *"and I think that we might*
Move his body and place it somewhere dignified."
"That would be a mistake." Sherlock Holmes signified.

"We should summon the Constable without delay,
Though I fear we must wait till the first light of day;
To ride over these Moors, no one should in the night,
For we do not want anyone sharing Will's plight."

"There might be more clues to be had in this shed,
Although many were marred when Miss Kathy had fled

And returned with the neighbours who ran to where Will
Had been found, dead and battered, just lying there still."

"He wasn't killed here, but somewhere on the Moor
I believe, for I cannot see blood on the floor.
I do not know what type of a monster Will faced,
But his body's been moved and deliberately placed."

"Deliberately placed? Do you think that is so?"
Asked Watson who'd said all the people should go
To their homes and let Sherlock examine the scene
And to leave him alone and to not intervene.

"I know he was placed after he had been killed
Somewhere else." stated Sherlock. And Watson, now chilled
By the thought of some psychotic madman at large,
Said, *"Perhaps we should wait for the Law to take charge."*

"We've been asking for that, all us folks on the Moor
But all the Law did was to send out some boor
Of a Sergeant or something who said we were mad,"
Said Jones in reply, *"then he went – we were glad."*

"So we thought of Sir Henry of Baskerville Hall
But at this time of year he'll not be there at all
For he closes the Hall –in the Spring he'll return -
A wintery Dartmoor's a place he would spurn."

"The Hall is closed up but some fellow's employed
To see ncthing is damaged or even destroyed
By the storms which beset us – he comes every two weeks
Although few people see him – it's seclusion he seeks."

Jones had not gone on home but had stayed just outside
Of the door of the shed in case he might provide

31

Anything Sherlock needed – he'd stay at his post
In the cold where felt he was needed the most.

"Come in, Mister Jones, it's a quite bitter night.
I'd asked others to leave but, of course, it's alright
If you sit on that bench to your left and not pace
All about for, you see, there are clues I must trace."

"Is there anything, Holmes, which might pass for a clue?"
Enquired Watson, who hoped that Sherlock might construe
Just some hint of the reason Old Will had to die -
Could Holmes, all those Satanic notions, belie.

"His boots are quite new, but a low muddy stain
Says he might have been walking outside in the rain;
He's not been on the Moors for, if that had been so,
They'd be both caked with mud. So, where did the man go?"

"They're largely unmarked on the tops, and the wear
On the heels and soles is so small I would swear
That they've only been worn for an hour or less;
But what this might mean, I'm unsure, I confess."

"The streets, here, are cobbled and mud's rarely found
Like it is on the Moor where the stuff's all around;
When one walks in that place one can rarely escape
The need to give both boots a vigorous scrape."

"When we first saw the body, one arm was outstretched
And I'm sure, if it isn't a little far-fetched,
That his forefinger pointed toward the shed door,
Or out into the yard, or beyond to the Moor."

"Take that lantern, we'll see if there's something outside;
Perhaps there'll be a clue to be found to provide

One more strand for that rope which is richly deserved
By the fiend who has done this and left us unnerved."

Outside crept the three to the yard where they saw,
In the light of the lantern, a leg with a paw;
Then another, then four and a torso and head -
It was one of Will's dogs, all dismembered, quite dead.

"That horror, that fiend, that abominable beast!"
Shouted Watson, not caring who heard him the least.
"Will the thing never stop? Who'd do this to a dog,
Or a man, for that matter? This fiend I would flog."

Then the horror compounded as Holmes shouted, *"There!*
"Bring that light." his forefinger outstretched, pointing where
Lay the second of Will's faithful dogs all displayed
Like the other, dismembered – Watson was dismayed.

"I am at quite a loss for how I might express
The emotion I'm feeling - I truly confess
That I'd gladly take up any axe I could find
And then doubly pay back this evil in kind."

"No doubt, most who have seen this would feel that way too,
Although, axing a suspect, we just cannot do."
Replied Sherlock who added, *"Random, this is not -*
Something else is behind this – some devious plot."

"We must question Miss Kathy - I know she should rest
But, more than any other, she may hold the best
Information on all these despicable acts
And, though she may not know it, she may have more facts."

Holmes and Watson and Jones, to Will's house, then returned
And, to question Miss Kathy, Holmes intellect burned;

He required more facts, his great mind was on fire.
But had she the answers the Sleuth would desire?

"Gently!" said Watson, *"Her emotions are brittle.*
If you want information, go little by little.
Her state is quite delicate. Holmes, understand
That her sanity's just holding on by a strand."

"I can see that," said Sherlock, *"I won't push too hard,*
But the things which we saw in the shed and the yard,
And what Jones has described, require action decisive -
My questions, therefore, must be somewhat incisive."

"Alright." agreed Watson, *"Here's Miss Kathy now,*
So recall what I said – no more will I allow."
Sherlock then took her hands and said, *"Kathy, My Dear,*
I must ask you some questions – some hard ones, I fear."

"Go ahead, Mister Holmes, ask of me what you will,
For I must be of help as my thoughts won't keep still."
Said Miss Kathy, unable to settle her mind,
"Ask the harshest of questions – you won't be unkind."

"I must ask if your father had things he might hide
From his past. I seek facts and don't wish to deride
A good man's reputation or bring him ill-fame,
But, might he have had secrets of which he felt shame?"

"Did he speak of a problem - of something gone wrong?
Did he have any items which did not belong
To himself or his work? And had his mood altered?
When starting to speak, had the man ever faltered?"

"Also, had he had dealings with anyone new,
Someone you'd not seen before, someone who drew

Your attention? If so, then, tell me, you should.
And tell me about his new boots, if you would."

"Mister Holmes, my good father's new boots were a gift
I had recently bought. He was not a spendthrift
And would wear his old jacket all ragged and torn,
But those boots, Mister Holmes ... they had never been worn."

"They were given to him only one fortnight back,
For his birthday, you see, they were shiny and black;
When he left to fix fences or drains or whatever,
He'd said he'd not get them all muddy, not ever."

"So he left them behind, 'neath the bench near the door
When he went to go trudging out onto the Moor;
From that day, I'd not seen him, that is, till tonight
When I found him – it gave me a terrible fright."

"Why on Earth was he wearing those boots? If he'd crept
In the house late one night, he'd have worn those he kept
In the shed to change into from ones caked with mud -
Mister Holmes, I heard nought, not a creak, not a thud."

*"Why, indeed?"*agreed Sherlock, *"And would he have not,*
On returning back home, come inside for a hot
Pot of coffee or tea to warm up his insides?
Also, where are his wagon and horses, besides?"

"Continue, Miss Kathy, think long and think hard.
Have you seen any strangers outside in the yard?
Did your father make comment in passing on some
New arrangement which wasn't entirely welcome?"

"We have not seen your father's old boots anywhere,
Though the one's he'd change into were spotted out there

35

In the shed, near the door, just as if standing guard
And awaiting your father's return to the yard."

Miss Kathy thought hard, although very upset,
And was trying so hard not to give way and fret;
Of her father's demise, she would not wail and cry -
She wanted to help Sherlock Holmes find out why.

"There was that new fellow at Baskerville Hall
But, what Father had called him, I can't quite recall;
It might have been Hardy which he had been saying -
Father didn't know at what Sir Henry was playing."

"Well, that's what Father said – so, the fellow, I took
To be not very good at his job – then he shook
Off my question about what the fellow had done
But said something on needing to speak to someone."

"Father said he'd been up fixing gates in the fence
Of our old homestead which, in a lengthy absence,
Had come loose in a gale – and although any stock
Had been moved, he would need a few pens he could lock."

"That fellow had been there – it's shelter he sought -
Father said that his first name, or so he had thought,
Was a little like Lawrence, or Maurice, perhaps
Or another name common to so many chaps."

"I gave it no further thought - it was just a remark;
But of what Father meant, I am quite in the dark.
Do you think, Mister Holmes, that this fellow's involved?
Do you think he might help get this mystery solved?"

"Well, Perhaps - perhaps not." replied Sherlock who then
Said, *"We should confirm his name and determine just when*

He commenced at the Hall and for what he's employed
And what freedom of movement the man has enjoyed."

"These are two facts to work with and, more, there may be,
And, when added to slaughter and murder, make me
Think that some great diversion is now underway
But, from what we're diverted, I cannot yet say."

"We must seek out this fellow at Baskerville Hall
Though it may well emerge that he's no help at all;
The man could have some knowledge he may care to share
Or, of recent events, he may be unaware."

"There is no more to do on this terrible night -
We must summon the Constable here at first light.
I suggest we retire – get what sleep we can.
Jones, it's alright just to cover the man."

"I'll do that," replied Jones, *"for Old Will was a friend,*
But a friend who has come to a terrible end.
I do understand we must leave things intact
Till the Constable comes, or for longer, in fact."

"As it's back, I will get my fast carriage hitched up
At first light and then, after a really hot cup
Of a really strong brew, I will be on my way
To get Constable Kent and hear what he might say."

THE CALL

The Police were too sparse on the Moors to present
Any major deterrent, but Constable Kent

Was on duty most days in a village nearby -
He had little to do, little reason to pry.

So it came as a shock on the day Jones arrived
With a story of murder – so far Kent had survived
On the odd bit of theft and the odd drunken fellow -
The latter he'd keep in a cell so he'd mellow.

Although theft was more serious, Kent often found
That, as often as not, he'd find, lying around,
Any goods which were stolen were often misplaced
By their owners who'd end up a little red-faced.

On occasion, however, a serious breach
Of the peace would have citizens trying to teach
Kent his business – they'd want action, drastic in scope,
Involving a gibbet and a long piece of rope.

On occasions like these, Kent had orders to quell
The mob's anger by saying he'd send off and tell
The Police at Headquarters that, come, they now should,
And detectives from there would then come if they could.

To a stupefied Constable Kent, Jones would tell
His strange story of murder and symbols from Hell;
Kent took down the details, wrote a message to send
To Headquarters, with one extra bit to append.

Kent's telegram listed each major aspect
Of the terrible crime but took care to eject
Any reference to Satan which Jones may have made -
Had he not, he'd receive an official tirade.

It said, "*Murder on Moors, please assist if you can.*
Victim Abernathy – well known local man.

Gunshot detected but body defiled.
No suspect as yet although villagers riled."

"Proceeding to scene but await your reply.
Have standard instructions as guide – will comply."
His appendix, however, would make them all sob:
"Sherlock Holmes has arrived and he's right on the job."

Well, Headquarters read over this message from Kent
And decided detectives should promptly be sent
To the Moors to investigate, fully, the crime,
And prevent Sherlock Holmes getting credit this time.

"Kent's been running around more than usual, I see,"
Said Inspector Dundas, *"And I see he's been free*
With his use of the telegraph; doesn't he know
That costs money – a letter is cheaper, though slow."

"His reports," said the Sergeant on duty, *"have been*
Overlooked and ignored, but the fellow is keen
To attend to his duties – the man's not a fool
And, by correspondence, he gets top of some school."

"He does what?" said Dundas, *"Well, then why, on the Moors*
Is the man chasing drunkards and banging on doors
And delivering summonses? We should have the man here
And not running around on those Moorlands, austere."

"Well, in truth, I can say, if I may be so bold,"
Said the Sergeant on duty, in tone rather cold,
"He's resourceful and clever, our Constable Kent,
And, though he may not like it, he goes where he's sent."

"His pay is appalling, his lodgings are grim,
And he can't see much future for someone like him

When he's stuck on the Moors with no hope of a change;
If we keep him much longer, I'd think it quite strange."

"His enlistment is finished this year, I believe,
And the fellow assumes there's no more to achieve
On the Force, so he'll go, just as soon as he can."
Dundas shouted, *"Why haven't we known of this man."*

"It's all in the reports," was the Sergeant's response,
"And out on the Moors, Kent, I'd not long ensconce.
But my stripes are held on by some thin cotton thread -
If I speak out of turn, I'll lose them, and my head."

Meanwhile, Kent and Jones had set off on their way,
Kent wondering what the detectives would say
Of his message of murder and villagers riled.
Would it stir them to action or would it be filed?

He had saddled his horse and had tethered it to
The rear end of the carriage - he knew he must do
All he could at the scene of the crime, and then go
Right on back to his post – he just couldn't say *"No!"*

He had no way to know but too much time to think
About whether this case would push him to the brink
Of discarding, forever, his uniform, blue -
He thought his resignation was long overdue.

But rather than dwell on a new occupation,
He considered Old Will and his sad situation;
He was eager to meet the world's greatest detective
And gain, if he could, some of Sherlock's perspective.

And, so, on their arrival at poor Old Will's shed,
They were greeted by Sherlock – Watson was in bed

For it had been decided to let him sleep on
All serene and quite peaceful, in oblivion.

"Mister Holmes - pleased to meet you." said Constable Kent,
"Your presence is welcome, in fact, heaven-sent.
I'm here all on my own and I do what I can
But the area's huge and I'm only one man."

"I've been trying to get some assistance to find
Who or what on these Moors is the evil behind
All this slaughter of animals, to no avail -
I can't do it alone, but I don't like to fail."

"And fail, you shall not, if my help, you'll accept.
You strike me as the type who is rather adept
At such work." declared Sherlock to Constable Kent,
"Are these absent detectives just useless or bent?"

"Well, they're neither, I'd say," replied Kent, *"they can do*
Just so much, but it seems they are loathe to come to
These mysterious Moors, so incredibly strange,
And where Nature itself seems to go through a change."

"I'd suggested the Army might help us to trace
The offender, but was told that, right into my face,
They would laugh before throwing me bodily out
Of the barracks and sending me off with a shout."

"The rules are quite different, the people distinct
From the rest, and have ways which, elsewhere, are extinct;
And when they try to question a Moor resident,
They will find a straight answer's a novel event."

"Well, that's not unusual." was Sherlock's reply,
"A detective expects that not all will comply

With his need to gain knowledge of what has transpired -
A great deal of patience is what is required."

"When his knowledge is little and he needs a lot,
He must ask many questions until he has got
A quite general idea about just who was where
And, just as importantly, who wasn't there."

"He must test what folks tell him, find what to retain
And what he can discard; then with facts which remain
Form a working hypothesis, fairly exact,
But never on just one convenient fact."

"One must never take things at face value, My Friend,
Which is why one must never overtly offend
Any witnesses who have, so far, hesitated
To come forth – they're no use if they're alienated."

"So, let's get to the bottom of all these outrages -
They're surely connected but, in several stages,
We'll ask and we'll test and the truth will emerge
As the lies dissipate and the true facts converge."

"Out here, you're respected; those detectives, less so;
We are quite few in number and, so, must forego
Any comforts we'd crave – to gain facts, we must strive -
All before the official detectives arrive."

"Even more so, now that a man's life has been taken."
Waded in Doctor Watson, now finally shaken
From slumber; and adding, while scratching his head:
"Had they acted when called, Old Will might not be dead."

"Doctor Watson, you're up, so meet Constable Kent.
He's the only policeman who's been on the scent

Of whoever's been slaughtering animals and,
Now that we've a murder, he must be on hand."

"Glad to meet you, young Constable. Holmes, you're a cad.
For, although my long sleep was the best that I've had
In a very long time, I still should have been called
To assist as I might – I am truly appalled."

"Your help wasn't needed till Jones had come back
Bringing Constable Kent so we might start to track
Down whoever committed this dastardly crime -
You needed the sleep – we'd have roused you in time."

"Well, I've tested the porridge Jones left in the pot,"
Said Watson who added, *"It's still rather hot.*
Perhaps it would be prudent to eat what we can -
He, who wouldn't eat now, is a quite foolish man."

"Quite so, Doctor Watson, remember those ribs -
They'll be no good at all sticking out like the jibs
You might find on a ship that's about to set sail."
Declared Jones, *"Everybody – fill up without fail."*

So, everybody filled up, and then Constable Kent
Said *"Here I have business."* and so they all went
To examine Old Will and his dogs, dead and cold.
Sherlock said, *"I have facts, if I might be so bold."*

Sherlock freely divulged all he'd seen and deduced,
Though, so far, a hypothesis he'd not produced;
"There is no time to waste; we must go to the Hall
And see if the fellow there's involved at all."

Kent added, *"Check out that old homestead where Will*
Said the fellow had been – he just might be there, still;

Or there may be some clues which might point to the man
That we seek – or, at least that's the start of a plan."

"That should be done right now, but I have to be back
At my station this evening so, time, I would lack
To do both," quite reluctantly, Kent then declared:
"I must see how my call for detectives has fared."

"I must be at my post for that message, and then
We'll find out if help's coming and, hopefully, when.
When I know what's afoot, I'll return with my horse,
Alone, or with colleagues expressing remorse."

While Sherlock and Watson and Jones all set out
For the Baskerville Hall, alone Kent set about
All his duties, official, describing the scene
Hoping that some detectives would soon intervene.

After gathering details and making a sketch
Of the scene, he remarked he'd be hoping to fetch
The official detectives to investigate,
Hoping Will wouldn't further deteriorate.

"It's my head if I move him," said Constable Kent,
"So I hope this cold weather will simply prevent
Poor Old Will's broken body decomposing right here."
But those from the village made comments, severe.

"He deserves our respect and, to move him, I should
To a dignified place, and I would if I could."
Declared Constable Kent, *"But my two hands are tied -*
"My instructions are such that they can't be defied."

Having made his arrangements, Kent set off to find
If a message was waiting for him far behind

At his small police station – *"They must soon respond;*
If they don't, then the killer may simply abscond."

As he trotted his horse on the slippery road,
Kent prayed that the detectives would help with his load
Which he knew was a thankless and difficult task;
He needed them here. *"Was that too much to ask?"*

So, upon his arrival, he darted inside
Having taken the steps in a long single stride;
An envelope sat in the tray labelled "IN" -
Had he been denied or did he have a win?

Well, the message within said that he was to ride
And determine if someone was dead, then provide
All the relevant details which he could discern
And then tell them if there was some cause for concern.

Simply fuming with anger, then Constable Kent
Scribbled out his reply and he then had it sent
To his doubting superiors saying that he
Could confirm Abernathy was dead as could be.

"Doctor Watson, a man militarily trained,
Has examined the body and duly explained
That the victim was shot in the back of the head
And had injuries done to him when he was dead."

Just a few minutes after that message was sent,
He received a reply which had simply said, *"Kent -*
Doctor Watson, to help, has not been authorised -
He should not touch the corpse – it will get compromised."

Again, Kent was fuming – he slammed his hand hard
On the bench, while exclaiming that he should regard

This directive received as a definite sign
That the time was at hand when he'd have to resign.

His enlistment, however, in two months, would end
So he needn't resign, he'd just formally send
In a notification he'd not re-enlist
And, to give graphic reasons, he'd simply resist.

Then, from Headquarters, one further message arrived
And it said the Police had been somewhat deprived
Of sufficient resources to respond that day
But, tomorrow, assistance would get underway.

"Well, that's better than nothing, I have to suppose,
But I thought that if ever the need once arose
For Headquarters to, such a danger, respond,
They'd assist me at once – I thought we had a bond."

"I will now have to wait till the train will arrive
After noon of tomorrow, though this will deprive,
From the eyes of detectives, a scene which is fresh
And I don't wish to think on the state of Will's flesh."

"I have what Mister Holmes had described of the scene
But, if I dare repeat it, I'd then contravene
All my orders from Headquarters. So, should I stand back
With my hands on my hips like a half-witted hack?"

"I'll write out my letter to say I've decided,
The Force, to depart, although I have provided
The full and complete summary it might need
If, to ever replace me, it chose to proceed."

But, away on the Moor, Sherlock, Watson and Jones
Had arrived in the carriage, which jarred a few bones,

At the Baskerville Hall where they hoped they'd unmask
The mysterious man at his dubious task.

As feared, he was gone and the place was deserted.
Could Sherlock's arrival have somehow alerted
This person of interest and made him take flight,
Or was he just away for another fortnight?

They were there, so they made it their business to see
If the fellow had been there to warrant his fee
That Sir Henry had paid him – the Hall was intact
But the wall 'round the gardens was damaged, in fact.

A large tree branch had fallen and damaged the wall
But there seemed to have been no repairs done at all;
"From the state of that branch," Jones occasioned to say,
"The thing's been down a month if it's been down a day."

"The wood is discoloured, the sap is quite dry,
And, if I was Sir Henry, I'd like to know why,
If that fellow was checking each fortnight, how could
The wall still be damaged for, repair it, he should."

"My suspicion increases," said Sherlock, alert,
"For with this breach of duty, distinctly overt,
More questions emerge with no answers received -
He must be a suspect unless we're deceived."

"But we do need more facts, so we must look around
And see if there are traces of him to be found;
It's crucial we know if he's been here or not
For, if he's been here, then his trail may be hot."

"This fiend who's been slaughtering animals, and
Then has murdered Old Will, may well still be at hand;

For he's needed a base where nobody would look
To attend to those evils which he undertook."

"If we only knew why he would do all those things;
For the work of detectives, I've often found, swings
On them knowing the reason the crime was committed.
It's a mystery, so far - that much must be admitted."

The three peered through the windows of Baskerville Hall
But saw nothing amiss, nothing undue at all;
A search 'round its perimeter gave them no clue
So a search further out would be, clearly, now due.

They searched through the outbuildings in hope that a sign
Would be found of the man, which, evil or benign,
Might expose the man's guilt or might clear him of blame
Of any wrongs done on the Moors, and of shame.

Many doors would be locked but some others just latched
And so Sherlock had Watson and Jones both despatched
To inspect their own sections while, pathways, he'd check
For some sign of their use, just some imprint or speck.

Holmes saw marks on a pathway–quite new, he had judged -
And a heavy iron gate had been recently budged;
And, though most had been spoiled by the night's heavy rains,
Holmes then saw the signs of large paw prints, and chains.

What those paw prints might be, he could not really say;
They were nothing like horses' and, far and away,
Far too large for a hound, even one which they faced
Just a few years before and which Mortimer traced.

But the shape and the size of the chain was distinct
And Holmes had to fight hard against every instinct

To imagine a hound of gigantic proportions -
Those paw prints, however, had many distortions.

So he measured the prints just as well as he could
And searched further around with the hope that he would
Find some further imprints, but found little of use -
In frustration, he felt just a little obtuse.

Jones searched through the barn but found nothing to show
Anybody had been in the loft or below;
And, nearby, at the stables where horses were kept
But which now were deserted, inside Watson crept.

The scene Watson found made his flesh start to creep -
A pentacle, topped with the heads of five sheep
At each apex, was drawn on the bare stony floor -
A sign that great evil had come to Dartmoor.

"Come Sherlock! Come Jones! Observe, here on the floor,
The sheep's heads and pentacle; and there, on the door,
There are many deep scratches no horse ever made -
I fear our missing fellow might well make the grade."

"I fear you are right," Sherlock had to agree,
"But whatever has been here is now running free
And may well get away unless we can act fast -
If we can, we may capture this madman at last."

"We must go to find Kent and tell him what we've found -
We must gather our forces and then run to ground
This most evil of fiends before he gets away -
If he does, I fear that he'll return here some day."

"Jones, can you think, from the knowledge you hold,
Is there some ancient lore or some legend of old

Which might halfway explain what we've seen in this place?
Is there some ancient rite that you're able to trace?"

"For whoever is doing this must have a plan
And, if that would be so and, somehow, if we can
Find out what he'll do next, we may set him a trap
Which he may well fall into, then hear it go 'snap'."

"Then we'll have the man, cold, and he'll pay for his act
When he faces the Law which he'll find will exact
The supreme punishment that the Law can bestow -
Nobody will miss him, and some may well crow."

"But, what he'll do next and where that might be done
We must anticipate and, so, if anyone
Might have any ideas on these evil attacks,
We may catch him before he can cover his tracks."

Jones said he didn't know of a legend involving
Such acts; and, so, Holmes was no closer to solving
What seemed like a riddle, a puzzle to crack.
So how could he solve it? His mood was quite black.

"These attacks which occurred, of revenge, ring out loud
And it may be the fiend thinks he's done himself proud
By disturbing the peace of the Moors in a way
Which would leave folks in terror and utter dismay."

"The danger's still great for, although he's departed
From here, it could be that the fellow has charted
A new course for mayhem and murder elsewhere
On these Moors - we must stop him before he gets there."

"On the other hand, he may have fled well away
And has not the intent of extending his stay;

His abominable beast, though, he may just release
And, if that is so, then our dangers increase."

"I saw no signs of wagon wheels out at the Hall
No sign that the beast was transported, at all,
To some place where it might be contained in a cage -
If it's loose, then its hunger will turn into rage."

"But why was this done, all this killing of stock
And of Will Abernathy? Was it just to shock
Someone into submission? Who knows who that may be?
If I didn't know better, I'd say it was me."

"But if it was me, why would that be the case?
Why would someone want me on the Moors on a chase?
Only one could come up with a scheme so profound
But my evil arch-rival's no longer around."

"Your evil arch-rival? I'm glad he's no longer
Around – because, living, there would be no stronger
Contender for all these outrages committed."
Said Watson who'd not have the notion permitted.

"But what is the motive? asked Sherlock, confused
At the lack of some purpose for people abused
As they'd been on these Moors. *"Could it simply just be*
That somebody, somehow, is just playing with me?"

"That's a little far-fetched," Watson said to his friend.
"Why would anyone come to the Moors just to spend
Some uncomfortable months having animals killed
On the chance you'd come down so that he could be thrilled?"

Holmes did not have an answer for Watson, and yet
He was plagued by a notion he could not forget.

They all travelled in silence – Sherlock thought on the beast,
He knew he must kill it, or catch it, at least.

THE GATHERING

They returned to the village, awaited by Kent,
Who had, telegrams, on his initiative, sent
Seeking word of some animal going astray,
"If it's both large and dangerous, answer today."

He'd received a reply that a circus had closed
And had sold off its animals but had disclosed
That a lion and leopard, a bear and an ape
Had somehow been abducted – they could not escape.

This was way up near Oxford but it had been thought
They were taken by parties who naturally sought
To recoup what the circus left owing, so then
As there'd been no complaint, the Force called off its men.

Kent had made more enquiries and duly discovered
That two of the beasts had been quickly recovered
By creditors chasing those assets removed
When they had, by the courts, had their ownerships proved.

The big cats were located, but they had been sold
To a London zoo owner who said he'd been told
They'd been pets, of a sort, in a country estate -
He had ownership papers and got quite irate.

That accounted for two – Kent discounted the ape -
The teeth marks were clearly the wrong sort of shape.

This left only the bear but, at this time of year,
Would the beast hibernate and, in Spring, reappear?

"I'm not sure, Mister Holmes, but I think, the year 'round,
That a bear in a circus might surely be found
To perform for a crowd in some novelty show.
But, if they close for Winter, I really don't know."

Sherlock said, *"That is excellent work you did, Kent.*
Now, if we can act on this, perhaps we'll prevent
Any more of these outrages, but we'll need help.
A beast such as this won't go down like a whelp."

"Let's assume that this bear has been taunted until
All its inborn instincts for the hunt and the kill
Had come up to the surface where, once, they were quelled
And its traits of obedience, all but expelled."

"That paw print I found, and the chain marks nearby,
Could well fit this hypothesis and, so, it is my
Suggestion we go out in strength and destroy
What we fear is a bear. Have we guns to deploy?"

"I've a rifle here with me," said Kent, *"I'm prepared*
To go out on the Moors – you must know I've declared
My intentions to leave the Police Force quite soon -
But we should not go out for it's late afternoon."

"When Dundas gets the bill for telegraph, he
Will explode and might even come looking for me.
Let us hope, if he does, he'll come very well armed
For, when he learns our plans, he'll be very alarmed."

"We must start before dawn of tomorrow and trace
Any sign of the beast, and then track it and face

It together, in force, and destroy it before
It can seek out a refuge – this great carnivore."

Holmes responded: "*Your initiative seems more than many
Policemen possess, for I doubt I've known any
Who go to such lengths and defy a directive -
I feel you would make an amazing detective.*"

"*It's a dream which I've had since the first day I joined
The Police Force, but found that my time was purloined
By Headquarters, it seems, as they needed some clot
To be stuck in the Moors because others would not.*"

"*You might think, Mister Holmes, I should try, one more time,
For a reassignment to where serious crime
Needs a serious fellow to chase felons down;
But it seems that they look upon me as a clown.*"

"*As of now, I'll take charge of this hunt for the beast;
It's my duty, you know, for I will have, at least,
A policeman's authority as is set down
For emergencies under the rule of the Crown.*"

"*I will listen to those who have input to give
About how one might capture this bear, fugitive,
And its keeper, of course; but I'll have no derision
For I am the one who must make the decision.*"

"*Are we all, here, agreed? If not, speak up now.
But I've laid down the Law and I will not back down.
There are times I may delegate, times I may not,
And I don't need armed men putting me on the spot.*"

"*I agree, absolutely,*" said Sherlock to Kent,
"*We should do as we're told and should go where we're sent.*

If we go as a rabble, the bear may escape
And a few of us may not return in good shape."

"That more personal matter, keep fast in your head
Till the time when the bear will be captured or dead;
You must focus your mind, there are lives in your hands
And you must give your all as your duty demands."

"We'll talk when this business is over and done
For, with all of my contacts, I'll surely know one
Who might help you advance;" declared Sherlock to Kent,
"If not, then your leaving, they cannot prevent."

"I will write a short note on the back of my card -
It will introduce you to Lestrade of the Yard
Who is, far and away, the detective I trust
Over all of the others – to meet him, you must."

"I have nothing to promise but there's a good chance
That he'll take you on board and he'll help you advance
In your chosen profession – I know you'll do well
For, apart from your courage, you know how to spell."

"But, before we lose more of what light we possess,
You should gather your forces so you can assess
What you're able to take on this perilous task.
We're in need of small arms, so who is there to ask?"

"We have your trusty rifle and Watson's revolver
Which, I must admit, is a great problem solver,"
Said Sherlock, recounting, *"but we will need more*
For I fear that a terrible fight is in store."

Jones made out a list of the village's men
Who might well come along if they just were told when

They were needed to track this abominable blight
And despatch it as soon as they got it in sight.

"We've a number of men here - I count up to twenty -
With rifles on hand, and we've shotguns aplenty;
I'm sure most, perhaps all, will come with us at dawn -
They'll be ready to go, though a few may well yawn."

"I can vouch, Constable, for each man on this list
And I think there's no way any one would resist
Such a call to take arms and join us in the hunt -
It's quite dangerous work and they will bear the brunt."

"Mister Holmes, you should wait – we'll be back in a bit;
Kent and I will go 'round to find who can commit
To the time we will need, see their kits are prepared -
When they go on this hunt, the prey will not be spared."

"Doctor Watson, likewise, you should wait with your friend
For, when speaking to villagers, I'd recommend
It be left to the locals who know what's required
When seeking an outcome the Law has desired."

Into Jones' house, Holmes and Watson withdrew
While leaving the locals to sort out a crew;
Kent and Jones would then rally all men, fit and able -
They would then put an end to this devilish fable.

Off they went through the village – Jones spoke to his peers
Whom he asked to fall in as unpaid volunteers
On the hunt for the creature which threatened them so -
And, as he had suspected, nobody said No.

Kent told all about what they'd be seeking to find:
"A large circus bear of a quite savage kind

Which is possibly starving and willing to kill
Anything it might find and to then eat its fill."

"We'll leave at daybreak and head off for the Hall
But we'll turn off before it and rummage through all
Of that low scrubby land below Will's old homestead -
If it's in there, we'll flush it and shoot the thing dead."

"We will need to check up on the homestead, as well,
For there had been no chance to examine and tell
If some trace of the fellow was there to be found -
Mister Holmes will, no doubt, have a good look around."

"The cart horses, we'll leave at the homestead of Will -
Its stable's secure so the cart horses will
Be quite safe from the bear should it ever come back
Seeking shelter from all of us out on its track."

"We'll need some men on foot and some other men mounted -
If we work as a unit, we'll make ourselves counted;
We do not want lone wolves going after the beast -
We're not here to provide some wild bear with a feast."

"We'll have outriders stationed to safeguard our flanks;
Three men on each side to warn those in the ranks
Of impending attack or the thing taking flight -
With luck, we might have the thing bagged by tonight."

"I'll get word to my Station to bring right across
To this village, detectives and, maybe, my boss
If I still have a job – that is, if they arrive;
And, of course, that's assuming that I'm still alive."

"I've made sure, if they come, they will not be alone,
Nor will they be unarmed – the Force would not condone

My providing the bear with detectives for lunch -
They will come in a wagon and come as a bunch."

Holmes spent much of the night, with his map, wide awake
Marking sheep-slaughter points to see if he might make
Any pattern emerge – there were five points in total,
Their positions, however, were quite anecdotal.

None-the-less, he pressed on, did the best he could do
Helped a little by Jones who, at some point, had to
Say to Holmes, "*All those points are the best for tonight -*
Now I must get some sleep – we've a bear we must fight."

Holmes looked at the well-spaced pentagonal points.
Were they all simply random or were they the joints
Of a regional boundary, a border marked out,
Where a fiend with a bear might go roaming about?

"*Ahah!*" shouted Sherlock, "*why didn't I trace*
This before? It was staring me right in the face.
Holmes – you're a fool and a great dunderhead.
You should go after facts, not some phantom, instead."

"*I'll draw from one point to the next point plus one,*
And repeat this until the whole five have been done;
I'll produce, when I'm finished, an irregular
But profoundly definitive, five-pointed star."

Holmes knew now that this shape had been used as a hex -
Each triangular arm formed a grisly apex
At which sheep had been slaughtered and decapitated
When evil and madness had collaborated.

In the pentacle's centre, supporting each arm,
Five lines formed a pentagon right 'round the farm

On which stood the old homestead – the message was clear -
A message that Constable Kent had to hear.

Next morning, all rose before dawn – few had slept
More than just a few hours, while Sherlock had kept
A quite long mental vigil in front of the fire
Contemplating the prospect of outcomes most dire.

At first crow of the cock, Sherlock rushed to show Kent
What he'd found on the map and how he should have sent
An armed group to the homestead and not to the Hall;
"*I believe,*" declared Sherlock, "*we're fools, one and all.*"

Kent looked at the map and he saw in a glance
That they well might have missed a most promising chance.
"*Good work, Mister Holmes; it seems obvious now
But, in hindsight, of course, things seem easy somehow.*"

"*I do not think, however, this alters our plan
For, if we're extra careful, I'm sure that we can
Reconnoitre the scene and proceed if we find
That this fellow's deserted and left us behind.*"

"*The odds are, however, that he left just as soon
As he heard you were coming, the same afternoon
That he must have placed Will and his dogs at the shed,
Then, releasing the bear, from the district had fled.*"

"*His name may be Hardy - it certainly fits -
He's very determined and clever, and quits,
I presume, when he sees that we're getting too close -
But soon, of his own medicine, he'll get a dose.*"

"*Mister Holmes, we must rise and all be on our way;
'The game is afoot!' Doctor Watson might say*

In those vivid accounts which we read in The Strand
For which, even out here, there is always demand."

Six horses were saddled, two carts took the rest:
Kent reminded them all that he, while on this quest,
Was in charge and would have no one acting 'The Squire' -
If one did, Kent would come down with brimstone and fire.

"Jones says he would trust each of you with his life
And, so, I will do likewise; but if we're in strife
And I can't carry on, you're to follow the sound
Of his voice instantly to where-ever you're bound."

"Now, we're off to do battle – at the homestead we'll pause
While we stable the horses, and also because
Mister Holmes needs to check all around it for clues,
Like some papers or clothing or bear residues."

The carts lumbered off and the hunt had begun,
Each cart full of men and each man with a gun;
On each side, single file, three sentinels rode,
Their guns at the ready, for great danger bode.

Some men had their hounds tethered tight to each cart -
They did not want them causing a premature start
To the chase by detecting a scent very strange
And quite unfamiliar to hounds on this range.

An attack was unlikely for cover was thin
And the bear couldn't help hearing all of the din
Made by two sturdy wagons on rough stony ground,
Not to mention the bark of an impatient hound.

In an hour of travel they'd be at the gate
Of the homestead where they, although likely too late,

Would halt, then determine if someone remained
Or if somewhere inside, the great beast had been chained.

An armed group went gingerly into the grounds,
All guns at the ready, all leashes off hounds
Just in case the bear rushed, as a cornered bear might -
In a few minutes, though, someone shouted: *"Alright!"*

Holmes and Watson went forward with Kent at their heels;
"Mister Holmes, what you see or what even just feels
Out of place is important, so what time you might need
You may take; so, with diligence, duly proceed."

"As you go through the pens and examine each one,
We'll unhitch the cart horses and, when you are done,
We will lock them within and provide them with feed -
They'll have shelter and safety, as much as they need."

There were only four pens but, there, in number three,
Were some tell-tale signs and Holmes, down on one knee,
Looked at what he perceived as a massive blood spill -
Blood once surging hot through the veins of Old Will.

It was brown and was dry for the spill wasn't new -
It had been there for some time and, as Sherlock knew
From the way it had flowed to a pool from one spot,
It showed Will losing blood after he had been shot.

There were no other signs which Sherlock could discern,
No footprints, no remnants – this was of concern;
And so Sherlock moved into the next pen and saw
Bits of torn bloodied clothing, the print of one paw.

"Watson!" Holmes shouted, *"get Constable Kent.*
We're too late for Old Will but we have to prevent

Anyone going into the homestead for now;
Further evidence loss, we just cannot allow."

"I have given that order," said Constable Kent,
"And have said what would happen if anyone went
Through the buildings and grounds before you'd had the time
To examine the site and find clues of the crime."

"Our advance group was careful but, still, left its mark
On the scene of the crime, but you could not embark
On your mission until we knew there was no danger
From a big hungry bear or that sinister stranger."

"Quite so!" replied Sherlock, *"And now I must check*
Through the building to see if the tiniest speck
Of Will's blood can be found, which I doubt we will do,
But there may be some clues to what did this, and who."

On exploring the building, Holmes found there had been
Someone living there, though he hadn't been seen
Until Will, he assumed, came to fix up the gate
And, what he then discovered, had sealed his fate.

"Will's murder," he pondered, *"may not have been planned*
But, as he had been killed and the flames had been fanned
By the slaughter of sheep, the fact Will came to drift
Into view was a fiendish, fortuitous gift."

"A gift, quite unplanned, or had Will, all along,
Been selected for slaughter but came at the wrong
Day to fix up the gates which came loose in the rain?
Did Will suspect this fellow he held in disdain?"

There were no indications of who it had been,
And no clue to the man's whereabouts could be seen,

So Holmes said to Kent, "*Within pens one and two,*
You may shelter the horses – here, there's no more to do."

"*He has covered some tracks, but has left a wide trail*
So, unless we're all useless, we just couldn't fail
To detect it and, on to its maker, descend;
But each trail has led to a sudden dead-end."

"*I cannot see a motive, as yet, but I feel*
That this fellow's not lucky, he's just made of steel
And does not have a conscience – he murders at will -
He lives for excitement – he lives for the thrill."

"*Does he know that it's me on his case? Could it be*
That, somehow, the object of his anger is me?
There's one man I know who might think up a scheme
Such as this and then push it beyond the extreme."

"*But, of course, Moriarty's no longer around.*
If he turned up today, it would simply astound
Me and cause me to question the health of my mind -
I saw the man fall – I'm not stupid, nor blind."

THE HUNT

Kent assembled his forces, two horsed groups on flanks,
Himself mounted, of course, and the rest in the ranks
In the centre, on foot and with guns pointing low,
All loaded and ready with death to bestow.

The flankers, in threes, held a hundred yard gap,
Well spaced but supportive – the eyes of a trap

Which would push the bear forward until it turned back
To confront its tormentors stretched out as a pack.

Holmes, Watson and Jones would all keep to the rear
With ten paces between them, maintaining a clear
Field of vision between the two flanks and all those
In the ranks out in front – when in danger, they'd close.

Jones had his best rifle, a shotgun as spare,
But Watson told Sherlock he just shouldn't dare
Face the bear with a cudgel; Jones said, on the run,
"Throw that stick to the Devil – you may use my shotgun."

Watson had his revolver, *"That's all I shall need.*
But Holmes your old cudgel's not up to the deed
We must do – take the shotgun – it should be enough -
You are not going up against some London tough."

Kent called out the order for all to advance
As they all did with caution – they'd not risk the chance
Of them blundering onto a sleeping wild bear
For, if startled, a few would return worse for wear.

No rain was then falling though, still, over ground,
The going was heavy as many had found
That the Moor's claggy mud, in some places quite thick,
Would pull hard at their boots – each foot felt like a brick.

The breeze blew toward them - some luck there, at least,
For the hounds would detect the strange scent of the beast
While the noise the hunt made would be somewhat decreased
And its chances to find the bear largely increased.

Through the scrubland, the hunt found it hard to keep spaced
As desired –some were glad that the bear wasn't traced

Where the cover was thicker than they would desire
And only a few had a clear line of fire.

In an hour, however, the scrub cleared away
And the Moorlands stretched out - Kent then hastened to say:
"We should stop here a while, give the horses a rest
And, of course, those on foot can recover their zest."

"Then, before we move off, several horsemen will ride
On ahead to see what the terrain might provide
In the way of some cover a bear might seek out -
If they see it, however, they'll give us a shout."

"For now, get some rest; take some water and food -
It'll refresh the body and improve the mood
After trudging through all of that scrubby terrain;
But we all should be thankful we haven't had rain."

Fifteen minutes, it took, to replenish the strength
Of the hunters and, Kent, the commander, at length,
Called the hunt into action: *"Gentlemen, with remorse,*
It's to-foot for the walkers; the riders, to-horse."

And so it would go for the rest of the day -
They kept in formation as they made their way
Over ground which was pitted with mire and muck,
Through a dozen deep gullies but, alas, without luck.

They would circle around as they swung like a door;
Hinging out from the homestead, they swept though the Moor
Seeking signs of the bear or its keeper, depraved;
Finding none, it was rest which the hunters now craved.

To the homestead they turned as the sun settled down
On a pinnacle, distant, almost like a crown

Before dropping down to the horizon below
Where it ended the day in a dazzling show.

At the homestead, the horses, unsaddled, were fed
And then, to the pens of the stable, were led
To be housed for the night against bears and the chill
Of a bleak Moorland night and a morning wind, shrill.

In the homestead's old house, all the men would be squashed,
Dry and warm although hungry and largely unwashed;
But a fire was started and food was shared out
And, soon, a hot beverage was poured from a spout.

A mug of hot tea and a cut of cold meat
And a large hunk of bread was a most welcome treat
For the hunters when followed by tots of hot rum
And a host of tall stories which turned to a hum.

As the hunters hummed on, Holmes vacated the house;
Watson said, "*I'll come too - I will dream of some grouse
On a plate on a table with doilies and wine -
Mrs Hudson's cuisine is a treat most divine.*"

Holmes responded by saying, "*A divine treat, quite so.
But out here on the Moors, to such things, we say 'No'
Till our quarry is caught and it can be despatched -
To a man who is hungry, our food is unmatched.*"

"*It will make Mrs Hudson's taste heavenly - more
Than we've come to expect.*" declared Watson who swore
That, when hunger pangs gnawed at his insides, he could
Catch a feeble old draught horse and, eat it, he would.

"*Well, that may have just been on our menu tonight.*"
Replied Sherlock to Watson whose face betrayed fright

At the prospect of horse, old and stringy and tough,
On a sandwich, while shouting to Sherlock, "*Enough!*"

Jones heard the two talking and joined them outside
In the shed and confessed as he sat by Holmes' side:
"*I have come to join you for I know what's in store -
All those men will stop talking and then start to snore.*"

"*They are all of the type who can work hard all day
And relax in the evening and then fade away
To a slumber so deep you might swear each was dead,
Then awake with the sun, fresh in body and head.*"

"*But, alas, my poor ears are not up to the task
Of receiving that sound bred of fatigue and flask.
So, if you can stand me through another night's sleep,
I will try to doze on without making a peep.*"

"*You are welcome, My Friend. Though I really suspect
That tonight, while I sleep, I'd not even detect
A full dozen express trains with whistle, at speed.*"
Replied Sherlock to Jones, "*You are welcome, indeed.*"

In their room, rather small, a large cupboard, at best,
The three comrades laid down for a well-deserved rest.
They were free of pretensions to glamour and poise
But, at least, they were free of that terrible noise.

The bear had, however, been stalking all those
Who had set out to kill it, but warily chose
To stand off and await the advantage to swing
Toward it when it would, on a lone victim, spring.

It avoided the house with its twenty armed men
And it worked its way 'round to the stables and, then,

Clawed the door till it splintered and left undefended
The horses within on which it then descended.

It then clawed at a couple of horses which fled,
In an absolute panic, away from the shed
And the stables; but one had no chance to get out
And it looked for escape as the bear turned about.

At midnight, Holmes woke to the sound of great fright -
The horse in the neighbouring stable kicked right
Though a wall in its panic -it was screeching in fear -
And Holmes thought that, the snarls of a bear, he could hear.

A match was then struck and the lantern was lit
And Sherlock was so lucky to not have been hit
By the hooves of the horse, but Jones jumped to restrain
The mad horse, in its panic, from crushing his brain.

Right over its neck, Jones had looped a stout rope
And he prayed for the strength to just hang on and cope
With the terrified creature bucking wildly in fear
And kicking out wildly at all who came near.

But the snarling continued, the roaring sustained,
And the horse kept on kicking as danger remained
From the claws and the teeth of a beast bent on death -
The shrieks of the horse carried fear on its breath.

Holmes and Watson ran out and they spotted the beast;
It was up on its hind legs – ten feet at the least
From its feet to its snout – its roar was demonic
And would render most into a state, catatonic.

Watson grabbed Jones' shotgun from Sherlock, then fired;
The shot didn't kill it but had the desired

Effect of arresting its deadly attack -
He reloaded both chambers and handed it back.

"You've wounded it, Watson – it'll now go to ground
And I fear, in this darkness, it will not be found;
But if it can be wounded and blood can be spilled,
The thing must be mortal and, so, can be killed."

"Grab that lantern – we'll follow the trail of blood;
There's so much that is seems like a bright crimson flood;
But, be careful, we should not go rushing its way -
It's a dangerous beast that is hurt and at bay."

The pair followed the trail of blood with great care,
The Sleuth and the Doctor both greatly aware
That it was a mad creature which they were both nearing,
When they suddenly found themselves out in a clearing.

A small camp, they found, though it had been vacated
Just minutes before, and so Holmes concentrated
On checking its layout – it seemed far too grand
To be used by some roughs who might live off the land.

"This camp is a dummy," he said in his mind,
"It's like somebody erected some model kind
To show campers the proper arrangements one might
Make for textbook-style camping on some ideal night."

The tent had been staked in a manner precise
And the ropes were all new and the pots far too nice
And too shiny, by far, for a knight of the road -
Was it all there for Sherlock, by way of a goad?

Holmes admitted to Watson while viewing the camp,
"I suspect Moriarty – this all has his stamp -

And I'd not be surprised to learn that he might bring
Such a creature to do such a dastardly thing."

"He's teasing me, Watson; I feel him nearby
Even though I can't think of a good reason why
He would come to the Moors and, our Capital, shun -
To that fiend, Moriarty, great evil is fun."

"Great Scott!" shouted Watson, *"The man is long dead*
But he's still an arch-criminal stuck in your head.
Moriarty, the least of my readers recalls,
Went base-over-apex at Reichenbach Falls."

"Good Gracious!" said Sherlock, *"Do my ears deceive?*
Coarse language, perhaps, I'd expect to receive
From the mouth of a seaman, all grizzled and crass,
Not the lips of a Doctor like Watson, alas."

"Holmes – never you worry about my expression -
You have to get over this stupid obsession;
The Professor is gone and he's not coming back -
If he's mixed up in this, then this Doctor's a Quack!"

Holmes considered the Doctor and weighed out each fact
Of the matter and said, *"At that great cataract,*
He had plummeted downward, my evil arch-rival,
But I just cannot discount the fellow's survival."

"I was there, you know, Watson - I saw him fall down
But I can't say, for certain, the fellow did drown;
I can recall the moment – it's like a bad dream -
And perhaps the man lived and he floated downstream."

"There was never a body reported as found -
He's a wily one, Watson, perhaps gone to ground

In disguise so effective no one could detect it,
And he'll take his revenge when we all least expect it."

With his head in his hands, Watson vented frustration
Saying, *"Holmes, Moriarty is just a fixation;*
We don't need a body to know the man's dead.
We must look somewhere else for this demon, instead."

Then a rustle came forth from the brush up ahead
And the pair stopped at once in a moment of dread;
But that moment passed quickly - both hunters prepared
To do battle and neither had time to be scared.

Sherlock's shotgun was held at his hip, firm and steady,
And Watson's revolver was held at the ready;
A few seconds seemed hours, but then in a flash
From the bushes ahead something made a mad dash.

Then a mad snarling mass bared its teeth at the pair
As it rushed to defend both its life and its lair;
It snarls were ferocious, it had teeth of a giant,
But the sleuths stood their ground, both prepared and defiant.

At its pair of tormentors, the wounded beast rushed,
But the pair quickly parted to stop being crushed;
Sherlock took a wild shot at the snarling beast's hide
While Watson pumped six lumps of lead in its side.

The beast gave such a screech to bring demons to heel
And, while Watson reloaded, Sherlock thought to kneel
Between him and the beast just in case the thing reared,
When the group of armed villagers duly appeared.

Twenty men, twenty guns - twenty shots rang out loud
And our duo was lost in a billowing cloud

71

Of a thick bluish smoke as the barrels spat death -
And the beast gave a groan with its very last breath.

"It's the bear," shouted someone, *"but of such a size*
Which would be, for a bear hunter, such a great prize
To be worthy of stuffing and putting on show,
To tell stories quite lofty, to brag and to crow."

Sherlock said to those gathered, *"A night's grisly toil!*
The beast is now dead but there's one we must foil.
We presume he's the cause of Old Will being dead -
A bear couldn't carve pentacles into his head."

"Don't say it!" said Watson, in fear of his friend
Being made look a fool, so he moved to commend
All the villagers, gathered, and praise their resolve
And not, any of Sherlock's delusions, involve.

"Gentlemen," he said, gingerly, *"there is your beast*
But I'd say it's too tough to be cooked for the feast
Which must follow your victory on this foul night
When your act cleared the Moors of this terrible blight."

The group milled about the dead beast and agreed
That a celebration of their act was, indeed,
An idea which was worthy of putting in play
And they gave, all at once, a collective *"Hooray!"*.

Standing back from the group was found Timothy Jones,
His old rifle discharged, leaning up on some stones
And expecting that Holmes would have something to say,
But Holmes would be hampered from having his way.

Holmes tried to address them above all the din
But Watson said, curtly, as he butted in,

"Let the villagers go, let them all have their party
And, for pity's sake, please, don't bring up Moriarty."

"But the bullet hole, Watson, the pentacle made
By a knife in Will's forehead, the camp near the glade
Where someone had been hiding, I need to explain -
These had not been conjured up out of my brain."

Sherlock wouldn't let go, though the beast had been killed -
Watson said, *"Our job's done and you ought to be thrilled."*
But he then asked the question which gave him most pause:
"If the bear was the symptom, then what was the cause?"

Watson snapped: *"You know felons, the way that they think,*
But the honest folk here had been right on the brink
Of a madness which could, with a single word, manic,
Make the whole population descend into panic."

"We don't know what they'd do at a time such as this.
They are very well armed and we would be amiss
If we didn't allow their excitement to cool -
The man who would stir them is truly a fool."

"Sherlock, as a friend, and a friend that is true,
I can tell you, at times, you just haven't a clue
How to handle good people when they're under stress;
We must let them calm down and not face more duress."

"I agree, Doctor Watson, these people are good
But they're likely to fear what is not understood."
Said Jones, in agreement with Watson's remarks,
"If they act in a pack, there'll be bites worse than barks."

Dressed in blue, still on duty, was Constable Kent;
He's commanded the group which had finally sent

73

The Great Beast to its death –his esteem may have grown
But the able policeman had plans of his own.

He also agreed with the stance Watson took
And suggested Holmes would be unwise if he'd look
Any further for culprits – the Police would insist
That he should, with his casework, now cease and desist.

Kent would take down the names of the hunters who'd played
Their unwavering parts in the drama and stayed
At their posts when instructed – he would make a complete
Report of the hunt and, with hunters, replete.

He knew the official detectives would come
And take charge of the bear and the body, gruesome,
Of Old Will and then have a great deal to say
About how things were handled by him on the day.

He expected no praise and he sought out no glory
For initiative taken when solving the story
Of demonic beasts running loose on the Moors
And for chances he took chasing bears out-of-doors.

"Mister Holmes," he said earnestly, *"now you will find
A policeman's authority is of the kind
Which is high at one moment but then falls away
When the work has been done at the end of his day."*

*"Holmes, you know how this works - it is always the same;
So you must look upon it as simply a game
Which is played between parties which want the same end."*
Said Watson who knew who they ought to commend.

*"The detectives will come in a carriage tomorrow
Unless Kent can find two more horses to borrow;*

74

They will inspect the bear and examine Old Will
And then go on back home when they've all had their fill."

"An investigation, the preliminary sort,
Will be made and, thereafter, an interim report
Will then blunder its way to the Coroner's bench
And he'll tell the detectives their English is French."

"These detectives will, after a sizable edit,
Resubmit the report which will give all the credit
To those who weren't there and who had to be dragged
To the Moorlands well after our bear had been bagged."

"But, in time, I'll be able to give every fact
Of the case to The Strand in which we'll re-enact
Every facet on paper – the people will know
Who has done all the work and who's stolen the show."

"Back to Baker Street, Holmes – at dawn we'll depart.
That is, if Mister Jones can avail his cart
And his time to deliver us down to the station."
Watson said in a tone of resigned expectation.

"Of course, Doctor Watson, but that train won't arrive
At the station until almost Ten-twenty-five.
You may sleep in tomorrow – we'll leave about Nine
And, if luck is on our side, the sun may well shine."

"Nine it is, Mister Jones, and we'll be on our way."
Doctor Watson responded, *"The work done today*
Will, I think, close the matter for Holmes and myself -
It's a matter of record to place on our shelf."

"The official Police will investigate, now,
The events which occurred and, no doubt, find out how,

And by whom, Abernathy had come to be shot,
Then do justice by Old Will, as likely as not"

"I'm far too tired, Holmes, to go over this more.
When you're stubborn like this, it's a quite futile chore.
You can stay here all night or come back and be fed -
I'm too tired to eat, so I'm straight off to bed."

"As for Constable Kent, I can't praise him enough
For the man was a rock when the going got tough;
But he acted with tact and with great understanding
When people's emotions were getting demanding."

"Perhaps we can help him, if help he desires,
Or Lestrade may provide the outcome he requires.
This will all have to wait until some other day
For tonight, to my dreams, I am drifting away."

They woke up, the next day, to the sizzling sound
Of fresh bacon strips frying - this made them both bound
From their beds to see Jones leaning over his stove,
"We'll have a grand breakfast this morning, by Jove."

"We'll have eggs as you like them, flipped over half way
Or just sunny-side up, as some folks like to say;
If you like them all runny, you must speak up soon.
I can scramble them, too, so they'll look like the moon."

"I've a craving for salt on my bacon, myself."
Declared Timothy Jones reaching high to a shelf
To retrieve a small jar. *"Use as much as you wish,*
I'll just sprinkle a little right into this dish."

"I'll have fresh tea, directly; the kettle's near boiled;
Bread and butter and jam for the fellows who foiled

The Great Beast of the Moors, though it wasn't from Hell -
We can't thank you enough – have some pepper, as well."

"A breakfast for kings, Mister Jones, I declare."
Replied Sherlock while digging right in to the fare
Trying ever so hard to restrain the desire
To say what he thought of a culprit, most dire.

THE RETREAT

The trip back to London was rather subdued
For the thoughts of the Sleuth were intensely imbued
With the notion of some evil presence behind
The events on the Moors, and it preyed on his mind.

As the train rumbled onward, those thoughts were confused
As the lingering notion that he had been used
In some devious game Moriarty created
Grew large in his mind – he became quite fixated.

Holmes went over and over the facts in his mind
Thinking Fate, in this instance, had been quite unkind
And, perhaps, a bit nasty and rather contrary -
But, of Watson's response, he would be rather wary.

"If, indeed, Moriarty's come back from the dead,"
Pondered Sherlock as thoughts coalesced in his head,
"Then how would he know I'm the one who'd be called?
What if some other case might have had me forestalled?"

"Could that fellow we sought for the murder of Will
Have been playing a game which, at first, would instil

So much terror that folks would remember the time
When the Baskerville hound was revived for a crime?"

"Was it possible, even, that fellow knew how
Many folks on the Moors would, within them, allow
All those tales, superstitious, they've known all their days,
To defeat common sense and recall ancient ways?"

"Just the hint of an agent of Satan about
In the night would raise terror and cause folks to shout
About evil and horror and bar all their doors
Against those wicked forces which stirred on the Moors."

"I'd presume that my previous efforts suggested
That, if some evil beast on the Moors would be bested,
A summons to me would be answered post-haste
Whereas calls to officialdom could be a waste."

"Was it just a coincidence Will was found dead,
In a manner designed to cause panic to spread
Through the folks in the village, the moment we came?
Was Will just a pawn in some devious game?"

"Were those shoes he was wearing a herring so red
That it shone like a beacon so I would be led
To believing a game was in play, and someone
Left a clue which was, consciously, quite overdone?"

"Was the five-pointed star on his forehead for me
Or was it for the villagers, knowing they'd be
Pushed to utter distress and determined to act?
Perhaps it was meant as a false artifact."

"If a plot was conceived by the one I thought dead
At the Reichenbach Falls then, perhaps, I was led

Into some clever trap by this fiend resurrected
Who, somehow, has lived all these years undetected."

"When I look at the problem, no motive, I find;
The crime has no reward, no return for the kind
Of appalling atrocities seen in our week
On the Moors – I believe I have been far too meek."

"We have killed off the beast and dispelled any thought
That an agent of Satan was that which we sought;
That much, we have done but there's much more to do.
With this, is there no one whom I may turn to?"

"So! To recap, I believe Moriarty still lives -
He's a quite vengeful person who never forgives
Or forgets any slight or affront which is made.
There is no one, however, whom I can persuade."

"There were stock mutilated and then rearranged
In a manner which pointed to someone deranged
Like some agent of Satan directing events
To have panicking folks going off at tangents."

"Moriarty'd have known that, in time, I'd be called
And he knew that, as I'd be completely appalled,
I would rush to the challenge and view every clue
Which I would, as the master-sleuth, try to construe."

"Perhaps, I was drawn to the Moors so I'd fail.
He'd have planned, well ahead, each and every detail.
He would leave just enough to get into my head,
And on every occasion, be one step ahead."

"If I say nothing, now, he will just try again
Causing others to suffer much anguish and pain

As he sets me a trap using people as bait -
I know this will happen – I just have to wait."

"But nobody will listen to what I might say.
They believe I would spook the Moor folk, and they may
Go off shooting each other in ignorant fear;
Jones and Watson and Kent made this point very clear."

"The Police will go forth and search high and search low
But that guilty one's long gone – that much, I do know.
Moriarty, the victor, now swaggers and struts.
But who would believe me? My friend thinks I'm nuts."

Doctor Watson, for his part, was very relieved
To be headed for home for he truly believed
Sherlock needed another case right in his sights -
A nice wholesome murder would set him to rights.

London seemed very strange, although they'd been away
For no more than a week – Sherlock wished he could stay
On with Jones and pursue that phantom of his mind
Which, despite the Police, he could not leave behind.

In their Baker Street digs, Holmes and Watson dug in,
Sherlock, ever, the under-used Knight, Paladin;
He hankered for action, he longed for the case
Which would challenge his mind and end up with a chase.

When the cases he needed were slow to arise,
He'd sometimes taken action most thought was unwise;
In the past, he'd used cocaine at seven-percent,
But Watson denounced it and wouldn't relent.

And, so, Sherlock moped on, quite unable to cope
With this idleness, seemingly all out of hope

Of his ever convincing Watson to return
To the Moors – Sherlock, meanwhile, would stay taciturn.

Two weeks after the killing of Will Abernathy
Holmes opened a letter from Will's daughter Kathy;
"Mister Holmes." it had stated, *"I'm writing to say
That my father's inquest has been posted today."*

*"It will be in a week, Wednesday next, and will start
Right on Ten, so it says, on the official Chart
Of Proceedings, according to Constable Kent -
You'll remember the one for whom Mister Jones sent."*

"Watson!" shouted Sherlock, *"next Tuesday we'll catch
Our old train back to Dartmoor; I've had a despatch
From poor Miss Abernathy – at last, the inquest
Will be held – I must be at my absolute best."*

*"That inquest will be held to determine how Will
Met his death, and I don't think my tongue should be still;
They'll need witnesses, Watson, and they'd be appalled
If I didn't attend, for I'm sure to be called."*

Well, the inquest was held on the death of Old Will
And the Public attending sat quiet and still
As the evidence log was explained without lull
By a Sergeant, quite large, in a monotone, dull.

Then Medical evidence, the facts and the trail,
The official Examiner gave in detail;
*"A bullet wound found at the back of Will's head
Was the definite cause of the man being dead."*

*"Other injuries done to Old William had been
Made post-mortem and, I must say, I never have seen*

81

So much damage to muscle and flesh as was done
To this man, and, of bones, I found no intact one."

"I examined the bear and I studied its paws
And I measured the width and the length of its claws
And the size of its teeth and the bite they'd inflict -
My findings, I feel, no one could contradict."

"The claws of the bear fit the slashes on Will
And its teeth match the bites on Old Will better still;
So I'm confident that, of the wounds that were made,
Those claws and those teeth were the cause, not a blade."

"I have sought the opinion of experts upon
Large carnivorous beasts, and one from the London
Zoological Park said he'd certainly swear
It's a great North American Grizzly Bear."

"And the Natural History Museum concurred
As a pair of its experts had hastily spurred
To rush down and examine the beast, then declare
It the largest Grizzly of which they were aware."

"And the Grizzly Bear is a quite savage beast
And the experts had said they were not in the least
Bit surprised at the damage inflicted on Will
For that bear is a beast which is born just to kill."

"I cannot say, for certain, connections exist
Between bullet and bear, and I have to resist
Making any assumptions that whoever shot
Mister Abernathy used the bear in some plot."

"I must not say more than the evidence shows
And, until he is caught, only one person knows,

*All alone in this world, if the bear was provoked
By the killer when some evil plot was invoked."*

The Official Examiner, though, had omitted
To give an account of the outrage committed
On poor Old Will's forehead - the five-pointed star -
The Mark of the Devil – the Satanic Scar.

It was thought that to give an account of that fact
Would be quite detrimental and even detract
From the objective thinking of those who must now
Describe just what had happened and, hopefully, how.

So the fact was suppressed and it would not be aired -
The authorities feared events would be impaired
By the tiniest hint of some Satanic act -
They decided to render some delicate tact.

The inquest rambled on - points and details were listed
As custom and legal convention insisted;
That a dastardly crime was committed, was clear;
Now, the Coroner's verdict, the Public would hear.

Then the Coroner spoke and his verdict was given -
*"A large Grizzly Bear, by some means, had been driven
To make an attack on the body of one,
William Abernathy, after death had been done."*

"And I find that his death, by a gunshot, was caused."
Then before going further, the Coroner paused
Before saying, *"The evidence before me has shown
It was done by some person or persons unknown."*

*"My findings, no doubt, will now put into action
The forces of Law which will, without distraction,*

Identify those who have acted to kill
So the Law can do with them whatever it will."

"This Court's now adjourned, that is all I can say.
This has been, I confess, a most distressing way
To sum up the demise of a most worthy man -
I would like to say more, but I don't feel I can."

Sherlock's mouth was wide open - the fellow was stunned
And he felt, by the Coroner, he had been shunned.
He'd been first to examine Old Will - had he not?
He'd been there when the bear had been fatally shot.

Had he not seen the pentacle carved on Will's skin
And the hole from the bullet which did Old Will in?
Had he not seen the camp which was clearly too neat?
Sherlock knew that he had so he rose from his seat.

Holmes, of course, had been desperate to speak up and say
That he knew who had done such a thing in that way;
So he said, *"That's not right."*, but nobody could hear
As the bustling crowd made its way to the rear.

Watson countered with *"No!"*, grabbed his friend by the arm
And said speaking would do him irreparable harm -
"The Police have the facts - they know how to proceed -
They'll find out who committed this terrible deed."

"They know it was murder; so the fiend will be caught
And then will, in due course, have a harsh lesson taught
On his person so others might witness and heed
That a felon must answer for each evil deed."

"I believe in that, Holmes – that a punishment must
Fit the crime it redresses, although I would trust

That the Law Courts of Britain would be quite humane
And, into an asylum, place someone insane."

"You have found the beast, Man - surely, that was your quest -
Let official detectives do what they do best.
Let them find who did this - let them dig and then delve
To find who's to be judged by good men, true and twelve."

"Back to Baker Street, Holmes, I insist that we go
And I will not accept it if you would say "No";
Our work here is done - there's a train we must catch
For, in London, there's always a crime set to hatch."

But Holmes, back in London, could not settle down
Because unfinished business was making him frown;
His mind, to new cases, he could not apply
Though, to Watson, it seemed that he just wouldn't try.

For two weeks, Sherlock languished until, in a flash,
He jumped up from his chair and he made a mad dash
To the street where he hailed the first cab he could find -
"The Police," he had thought, *"are all running 'round blind."*

"They must know what I know – my suspicions I'll tell
To Inspector Lestrade who'll soon have in a cell
The most evil wrongdoer the world's ever known
If he listens to me and believes what he's shown."

A Hansom was called and then, in, Sherlock hopped
Like a man on a mission who wouldn't be stopped;
He then said to the cabbie, *"Scotland Yard if you please -*
Use your whip to effect, this is no time to tease."

He arrived and he charged through the doors past the guard
And he shouted, *"I must see Lestrade of the Yard."*

"He's back this very minute," a Sergeant announced,
And when he appeared, Sherlock eagerly pounced.

"As you know, I was down on the Moors where there'd been
An occurrence which very few people had seen
As a huge evil beast had been set upon stock
And the folks of the region were sent into shock."

Lestrade listened and said, *"I have heard of that case -*
It seems some massive bear had been goaded to chase
Lots of livestock around, sometimes rip them to bits
With its powerful teeth and a great pair of mits."

Holmes said, *"That's the one, but there's more you must know*
For a man had been killed and a sign left to show
That his death was a warning-great evil persists
And would crush, underfoot, anyone who resists."

"There has always been evil," Lestrade then replied,
"But that evil is in every felon who's lied
And has cheated and robbed and, perhaps, even killed
To get rich without working, or just to be thrilled."

"That case on the Moors isn't one on our books -
The local detectives can catch their own crooks.
Now, to hear this My Friend might, for you, be quite hard,
But, Sherlock, this isn't a case for the Yard."

"We are up to our noses in cases galore
And the powers-that-be are not looking for more
To take on at this moment – especially those
Which that private agent, Sherlock Holmes, might propose."

"We do not need your help to find crimes we might solve,
Most especially if they might be crimes that involve

Some sensational theory – we know where you live
And we'll contact you when we need help you might give."

"But Lestrade," Sherlock countered, *"at least hear me out*
For I have information I'm dying to shout
From the rooftops to all who would listen and heed
Of the one who committed that terrible deed."

But Lestrade, overworked by the cases he carried,
Was rather annoyed at the way Sherlock harried
And tried, from his work, to cajole him away;
Lestrade would not listen to Sherlock that day.

"I don't have the time and I can't interfere -
If I did, repercussions could be quite severe.
I suggest you go home – leave police work to those
On the job and who'll bring that odd case to a close."

"Moriarty's the one!" Sherlock said as he stamped
On the floor with his foot while, with both hands, he clamped
On the forearm and wrist of Lestrade who said *"Don't!*
I have told you I can't, now I tell you I won't!"

"Moriarty is dead – you, yourself, have declared."
Said an angry Lestrade with his teeth almost bared;
"Now, before things get nasty, go out through that door -
I'll not go chasing phantoms on some barren Moor."

"I have spoken with Kent – I'm impressed with the man
And I'll try to do for him whatever I can.
He has mentioned to me you said some mastermind
Had the folks on the Moors all out running 'round blind."

Lestrade shook off the grip Sherlock had on his arm
And, to Sherlock, it seemed that he'd lost all that charm

Which he'd used upon many detectives, official.
Were his techniques, substantial, now just superficial?

The Police wouldn't listen; perhaps the Press would
And they'd sort out the problem if anyone could;
He would write to the Papers and give them his views -
After all, the Newspapers were looking for News.

So he took pen to paper and listed the facts
And the details of all the despicable acts
Which occurred and which had him, by people distressed,
Summoned down to the Moors and a creature, possessed.

He explained how he thought that it had been a trap,
An elaborate one, but a trap set to snap
And to snare Sherlock Holmes and perhaps get him killed
In a way that would have any vengeful type thrilled.

Well, the Times gave to Sherlock, a spot on page five:
*"A consulting detective claims there is, alive
And about on the Moors, a professor who fell
To his death long ago, but is now back from Hell."*

The Times' editorial staff had respected
What Sherlock had done in the past but detected
That something was wrong, so they printed enough
To acknowledge his claim, although others got rough.

Well, the tabloid newspapers went truly berserk
And they labelled poor Sherlock a fool and a jerk
For insisting that someone who'd been dead for years
Was the cause of the evil that brought folks to tears.

All their headlines were cruel – each had gone for the throat
Of the greatest detective and called him a goat.

They were fickle, capricious and seemed to forget
That he'd beaten almost every felon he'd met.

"Just what's Sherlock Holmes keeping under his hat?
Has his brain been replaced by some mischievous bat?
Has the poor fellow lost it? Is he one theory short
Of a story for Watson to write and report?"

"Holmes told us the Reichenbach waterfall swallowed
Some evil professor, and then later wallowed
In glory when he reappeared, as the danger
Had passed, with a story which couldn't be stranger."

"Now he says the Prof's back even though he had claimed
He'd been killed and his gang had been fatally maimed
After those who'd survived had been incarcerated
And, London, then safe, should be truly elated."

"Mister Holmes," it had asked, *"are you out of your mind?*
Is there some piece of evidence that we might find?
Your waterfall story sounds wetter and wetter -
Mister Holmes, the Public deserves something better."

Sherlock stuck to his guns and his principle, prime,
Which had served him, unswervingly, time after time:
"When all else is discounted, each fact and concept,
Whatever remains, I am forced to accept."

For some weeks he laid low till the furore subsided -
He couldn't see why he was being derided;
But the Tabloids lost interest, they found someone new
To attack just for having a dissenting view.

Baker Street seemed quite lonely and Sherlock felt strange
And he felt it was time that he should rearrange

All his records and papers in case clients called,
But nobody came near him and he felt appalled.

Sherlock's friends would avoid him - he wouldn't stay mute
On that subject he always tried hard to dispute;
He'd harangue brother Mycroft, Watson he'd bombard,
And he'd button-hole, weekly, Lestrade at the Yard.

Watson ceased writing stories to print in the Strand
As the publisher told him the Public's demand
For the exploits of Sherlock had fallen quite low;
As a friend, Doctor Watson would soften the blow.

"Holmes, you know people, they're picky and fickle;
They need something new that, their fancies, will tickle;
We may have exhausted their need to be shown
That superior minds have a life of their own."

"They could never inhabit that world where you live
So I'll stay my old pen and the silence will give
Them a rest from your methods, and something inane
Will then be their distraction from lives quite mundane."

"You should visit the South Downs, you've said it's the place
You'd retreat to if ever the time came to face
That event, once far off, when you'd hang up your hat
And proceed to raise bees and, perhaps, keep a cat."

"I would never suggest, for one moment, My Friend,
That your life of detection has come to an end.
But we must face the facts, as you'd surely insist,
And from contentious comment, now cease and desist."

"I will make some arrangements, just leave them to me
And, in just a few days, you will find you will be

On a train steaming rapidly out past those fields
Of our countryside where, from the heart, anguish yields."

"For the railway's a conduit of magic and peace
And the train's gentle movement gives mental release
As we're carried along and our thoughts start to lift
And to float overhead with our minds set adrift."

"They're the envy of many, our railways which track
Through the country, to take us and then bring us back
To wherever we want in our own happy nation,
Of course, that's assuming it's near a train station."

"Thanks to Stephenson, Watt, and Trevithick as well,
And don't forget Isambard Kingdom Brunel,
We can travel wherever we might feel the need
In safety and style and in comfort at speed."

"His family is French," uttered Sherlock, *"like mine.*
In some part, at least, through my maternal line
And Brunel through his father, an engineer, too,
Who had come to our shores well before Waterloo."

"Get away with you Holmes, that's not possibly right ."
Replied Watson, appalled, *"Would you cast a bad light*
On this country of ours? You just have to admit
That Brunel, through and through, was a definite Brit."

Sherlock said, *"I've no doubt, but there are in this land*
Many old family lines, both obscure and grand,
Which have origins, east, from the great Continent;
Don't forget, our dear Queen is of German descent."

"Poppycock, Sherlock! Why must you talk rot?
There's not one drop of blood which Her Majesty's got

In her veins that's not British – on thin, ice you tread
And there once was a time when you'd forfeit your head."

"I'm just saying," said Holmes, *"we might be British stock*
But it just oughtn't be such a terrible shock
To recall that those waves of invaders who stormed
To these shores long ago, our great nation, have formed."

"Just recall that we're Britons and Saxons and such
Also Normans and Danes and we all have as much
Right to call ourselves British – put the past well behind -
Crown Prince Eddy's half Prussian and he doesn't mind."

"Well, blather and blast, Sherlock, see what you've done."
Uttered Watson, red-faced, *"You've told me there's not one*
Single person residing in Britain today
Who's not come to these shores from a land far away."

"The point is, My Friend, that it just doesn't matter.
Our good Queen's grandfather, himself, was a latter
Day migrant, of sorts, to our Britannic bunch
And he couldn't speak English to order his lunch."

"The rolls of our Army and Navy display
Many names from our shores and from lands far away;
They take pride in their units, their flag and their nation -
They remember their roots, but it's not a fixation."

"Some are Dutch, some are German and Russian and Swiss,
They stand up for this land though, their old ones, they miss;
Most are fine and upstanding and tall in their ranks
And I, for all that, express my humble thanks."

"From our Isles, though not English, a great many fill
Up those ranks, straight and true, offering their blood to spill;

I know some come from Glasgow, Cardiff and Cromarty,
Though I don't know the source of the name Moriarty."

"That's it!" shouted Watson, "I'm buying that ticket.
You're batting, you know, on an old sticky wicket.
Moriarty has still got your brain in a fix -
It's time that you hit that old crook for a six."

"You've insulted the Queen and her son, the Crown Prince
And said things about Britain which just make me wince;
My patience, My Friend, is about to give way
So I think you should start for the South Downs today."

"So, prepare yourself, Holmes, you must make a new start.
You must ready your mind, and we know, as you're smart,
You will master the skills you will need when you don
Your bee-keeping apparel. A new game is on!"

THE DOWNS

Holmes responded, declaring, "Watson, you're quite right!
Perhaps Sherlock Holmes must relinquish the fight
And then start a new page in his own book of life -
We'll take leave of this city, its evil and strife."

"We will travel to Sussex, the South Downs are calling;
Though it's Autumn and soon all the leaves will be falling
And leaving each tree with its skeletal shape,
None the less, to those beautiful Downs, I'll escape."

"The South Downs form an Eden of which we may boast -
Where the folds of the Earth ripple down to the coast

To where cliffs, straight and white, from the waters, arise
And, where, every turn in the road brings surprise."

Watson made the arrangements for travel and lodging -
They'd depart in two days and would celebrate dodging
Those crowds in their thousands, that city of death,
And enjoy their new freedom, their freshness of breath.

Watson told Mrs Hudson - she felt rather sad
But she knew that, for Sherlock, his life had turned bad;
Watson said, "*I give Sherlock three months to shout 'When!',*
You should let out his flat if he's not back by then."

"*If he lasts till the Spring, the South Downs, he'll not spurn,*
But I don't think, his bridges, he's ready to burn
For a little while yet. For myself, I must stay
At my practice, but I'll see Sherlock safely away."

The train ride wasn't long, not two hours with stops,
But with one hour added when adding on hops
Which were made on a cart which was not made for speed -
It was pulled by a pony and not by a steed.

At a town, unpretentious, a village, perhaps,
The two tourists, in lodgings, undid all the straps
On their bags and prepared for an extended stay -
How long that would be, Watson just couldn't say.

But he hoped for the best - the best being forever
For Sherlock who swore, to return, he would never,
Unless to attend to the needs of a friend -
Otherwise, his old life, he declared at an end.

There were still a few hours of daylight remaining;
Neither Watson nor Holmes ever thought of restraining

The mutual desire of checking the lay
Of the land they had come to until the next day.

Watson thought he should gather some expert advice
And would offer to pay any reasonable price
To have Sherlock distracted from recent events
And was happy on finding some advertisements.

"William Wilkinson-Hugh, apiarist of some standing,
Three lectures, will give, which are not too demanding
At the village Church Hall, starting Wednesday at Six
With a field trip to follow – its date yet to fix."

"On consecutive evenings, you'll learn how to start -
How to fathom the science and master the art.
The First introduces the hard-working bee,
Its life and its limits, to each attendee."

"The Second shows how one should manage the hive,
Gather honey while keeping those workers alive.
The Third - how to market those jars full of honey
And how to convert all that sweetness to money."

"The Field Trip will show each attendee the ropes
And will merge practicality with all those hopes
Which had brought each to have extra knowledge imparted."
Watson was impressed - he must get Sherlock started.

Watson walked through the village – he needed to drop
Off some mail for delivery and also to shop
For a few small essentials – there, he'd ask, as he ought:
"William Wilkinson-Hugh, where might he be sought?"

Watson posted his letters, saw a shop he admired,
Crossed the road and then entered the shop and enquired.

The shop-keeper told Watson, *"Yes, I know him well*
And the way to his home is quite easy to tell."

"William Wilkinson-Hugh, Billy Bee to his friends,
Can be found at the house where the Market Street bends;
When you walk from the shop, turn left, walk a mile
And you're sure to find William out back with a smile."

"It's the big house with Wilkinson-Hugh on the gate;
Its three hundred years old, and a bit out of date,
But its charm's in its history, the family it's housed -
Though it's bees, nowadays, that get William aroused."

"So I've heard," replied Watson, *"thank you ever so much,*
It's his knowledge on bees that I'm seeking, as such."
Watson stepped from the shop, found that house full of charm
With the apiarist tending his miniature farm.

"Mister Wilkinson-Hugh, Doctor Watson's my name;
I've a friend, Sherlock Holmes – you might know of his fame.
If, too much on your time, it would not be encroaching,
I'd hoped you'd agree to some special bee coaching."

"I see, starting Wednesday, three lectures are given
At Six in the evenings for those who feel driven
To learn about bees and their hives full of treasure
For financial gain or just simply for pleasure."

"These, Holmes will attend – your field trip, as well;
I will do so, myself, for, although I still dwell
In midst of those millions which London contains,
My Practice is small and a colleague remains."

"Once a master detective, my friend would withdraw
From that calling and settle where-ever good law

Biding people are found – he finds order with bees -
He's past looking through keyholes while down on his knees."

"My friend would raise bees and, to learn, he is willing -
He has lots of time which is in need of filling
And is keen to get started as soon as he can.
Where bees are concerned, he's a definite fan."

"He's alert and he's clever and lives just to learn
And, to learn from the best, is something he would yearn."
Interrupting, the apiarist announced, hitherto,
"First things first, Doctor Watson –now, How do you do?"

"Forgive me, please, Sir – it must seem rather rude
To just barge in like that – I don't mean to intrude.
I am quite pleased to meet you–I got too excited -
I should not have come forward till I was invited."

"Tell me, Doctor Watson," said the apiarist, dryly,
"I would guess a detective would come on quite slyly.
Shouldn't he be the one to approach me on bees
Or does he collect data through his appointees?"

"The fact is," replied Watson, *"that Sherlock, of late,*
Has had setbacks and has had a lot on his plate.
He's a little dejected – he needs someone who
Will take charge of his life till he knows what to do."

"Well, working with bees can help get the man sorted,"
The apiarist said, *"if his mind's been distorted."*
William Wilkinson-Hugh, though, would dig a bit deeper -
"Would he be an apiarist, or a bee-keeper?"

"They're different?" asked Watson, *"They both need the bee."*
But the grizzled old apiarist did not agree -

"*A bee-keeper keeps bees to keep him steeped in honey,*
While bees keep an apiarist knee-deep in money."

"*The first is a hobby, a sweet one, it's true;*
The second's a business, so try to subdue
Thoughts that effortless money from bees can be gained -
An apiarist finds, to the hive, he is chained."

"*Just remember, the bee is a harvester, small,*
But so many fly out that they might gather all
Of the nectar they can from the flowers which bloom -
So many bee-hives will require so much room."

"*And, as blooms come and go, so the bees have to follow*
New flowers for nectar or hives will grow hollow
As honey is taken – a bee-keeper believes
That the bee enjoys working for us though we're thieves."

"*An apiarist, however, must attend to each need*
Of the bee and appreciates that it must feed
On the nectar from flowers and, so, like a groom,
He must move hives around to where new flowers bloom."

"*He's a farmer, in fact, and much work is involved*
And, to do what is needed, he must be resolved;
He'll look after his bees and keep them at their prime,
But the product is sweet and it's worth all that time."

"*You must realise, however, at this time of year*
There are very few flowers and it should be clear
That, if there are few flowers, the bees can't collect
Enough nectar for even their queen to detect."

"*Still, there's work to be done even when it is cool*
And the one who would neglect his hives is a fool;

'Nature knows best', it has often been stated
But that saying, I fear, could be much over-rated."

"Your friend has to realise bees are a calling
And, if he would answer, it would be appalling
For him to decide bees should fend for themselves
In their hives during Winter like miniature elves."

"I do take your point," blubbered Watson, astounded
That bees could engender such fervour, unbounded;
"I do think my friend would keep bees just to see
If he might, one day, breed a superior bee."

"What insufferable twaddle!" the apiarist yelled,
"If he thinks along those lines, I feel quite compelled
To refuse to assist such conceit in your friend -
If that's so, Doctor Watson, our talk's at an end."

"To think one could improve on a thing of perfection
Which Providence gives us is, clearly, rejection
Of all I hold dear and profess to be true -
Your friend, Doctor Watson, does not have a clue."

Watson, taken aback and a little offended,
Felt Holmes' need of bees should be strongly defended.
If he now showed respect in a manner quite pensive,
Might he gain the man's help by not seeming offensive?.

"Forgive my good friend – his mind is of the sort
Which demands constant use, but he'd never resort
To deception or lies – for the truth, he's alive,
Whether that be for justice or bees in a hive."

"He, too, believes Providence made him that way
And he'll stick to his mission till his dying day;

He would learn all the ways of this hard-working beast,
Be it ever so small, and not harm it the least."

"Well, if he's of that sort, I suppose it would be
Quite all right for your friend to get coaching from me.
You should bring him along – Tuesday, next, would be best,"
Pronounced Wilkinson-Hugh, "and I'll see if you jest."

Doctor Watson, a little surprised at the way
That the fellow had changed, simply uttered, "Tuesday!
I can't thank you enough, you are truly most kind,
And you may just have rescued a truly great mind."

Tuesday-next came along and Sherlock made his way
To where Wilkinson-Hugh would be working that day.
"Mister Holmes, you're expected." the apiarist called
To his new protégé, though his work hadn't stalled.

"I see that you're prepared with your gloves and your hat
With the protective gauze which is needed so that,
If you don't treat the bees with the proper respect,
They're not able to sting you, as you might expect."

"I'm removing the combs from the hives, you might note.
If I follow procedures, there's not a remote
Chance of me being stung – I have done this before -
And if I respect bees, I'll have honey galore."

"For the bees have to trust me, although there's a chance
They'll take me for a predator and take a stance
Of offensive defiance and emerge on the wing
And attempt to attack any skin they might sting."

"Being stung once or twice in each season's a good
Thing to happen, as workers have long understood

That the more one is stung then the less one reacts,
And the less one reacts then the less it distracts."

"But, of course, being stung by a hundred or more
Angry bees at one time would make one rather sore;
And the poison injected by so many bees
Is enough to bring many strong men to their knees."

"And even to kill?" Sherlock asked, *"For I've known,*
From my knowledge of poisons, a man who's full grown
Can sometimes succumb to the sting of one bee,
So a hundred would kill him. Would you not agree?"

"Well, there have been some cases where some have survived
Though it did take some time to get victims revived.
Some were never the same, some were better than ever,"
Said Wilkinson-Hugh, *"although, met one, I've never."*

"Come, we'll do what we can, though the season is folding;
You can start off your lesson this first day by holding
This bucket while carefully watching the way
That I scrape clean the combs I have here on this tray."

"There are few I must scrape for, now, flowers are few
And the bees must await more to come into view;
But there's work to be done, so much more than you'd think,
And, away from those labours, one must never shrink."

"Being late in the season, the bees now prepare
For the Winter when each flowering plant is quite bare;
And also, throughout Winter, bees must be protected
From cold and from being, by diseases, infected."

"But, in Spring, Mister Holmes, there's a glorious change
As all Nature revives and we must rearrange

All our lives, once again, to the needs of the bee
As each little hard worker prepares to fly free."

"So your life must be tuned to the seasons each year -
On this point, I would labour - I want it made clear
That you're wasting your time and good deal of money
If you cannot adjust – the life's much more than honey."

"You must come to my lectures, you'll learn quite a lot;
Come tomorrow at Six, and we'll start on the dot
At the Church Hall with pictures in colour to show
For the hall has its own magic lantern, you know."

"Then, on Thursday and Friday, again, right on Six,
There'll be two further lectures and then we will fix
A convenient time to go out in the field
To see just how an apiarist gets a good yield."

"Wonderful!" exclaimed Sherlock, *"I'll be there on time.*
I'll be seated before the church bell starts to chime.
I'm excited and just cannot wait to get started
For I'm on an adventure to places uncharted."

"Well, you'll soon have your bearings," the apiarist chuckled
As he took off his hat and his gloves and unbuckled
His heavy apron, *"So, prepare to set sail*
Just as soon as you've mastered each point of detail."

"If you come back tomorrow, you'll learn a bit more
And, if you can stay on, I might need help before
My first lecture, for there is so much to prepare -
You could be a great help if, to do so, you'd care."

"Care to, I would." Sherlock said with excitement,
"For the subject itself is sufficient incitement;

You are excellent company, forthright and frank -
And for me" being here, I have Watson to thank."

"An excellent fellow, a friend tried and true."
Declared Sherlock Holmes, trying hard to subdue
His emotions which seemed to be on the escape,
"Together, we've both come through many a scrape."

In the weeks that would follow, Holmes learned all he could
And he might have learned more if the cold weather would
Have only held off, or if he had decided
To follow his dream when he first was derided.

When it seemed Sherlock Holmes would, indeed, persevere
With his passion for bees, and it wasn't a mere
Case of simple escape from a wearisome life,
William Wilkinson-Hugh spoke of trouble and strife.

"Mister Holmes, I must tell you of trouble we've had.
It seems one of our guild, a despicable cad,
Has been killing our bees and destroying our hives -
Hives which, quite often, support many lives."

"We presume it was one of our group who has done
All this damage, but there is not one single one
Of us who we would think could descend quite that low -
How to capture the culprit – we really don't know."

"At our meetings, an air of distrust often lingers
And some, at each other, point reproving fingers
And often resort to quite bitter invective -
We could use the help of a private detective."

"Mister Wilkinson-Hugh, I'm the man that you need,"
Sherlock proudly retorted, *"for I am, indeed,*

103

A consulting detective, a private agent
Who can delve where policemen would never be sent."

"Yes. I've heard of your exploits, but you have retired,
Or so I've been told, because you had required
Great change in your life and you needed some rest."
Replied Wilkinson-Hugh to his energized guest.

"I'll rest when I'm weary," said Sherlock, defiant,
"But when on a case, I've the strength of a giant
Who will not be restrained or put off from his task.
Just give me the facts, that is all that I ask."

"The facts, you have heard, for I don't know much more
Than what I have told you. I don't wish to bore
You with trivial details and gossip malicious,"
Declared Wilkinson-Hugh, "for some types can be vicious."

Sherlock thought to himself, "Well, this is a surprise;
I'd imagined bee-keeping a calm enterprise
But I find, even, here, human nature prevails -
It's not only bees which have stings in their tails."

"On the South Downs I thought I'd be calm and composed
And would mix in with folks who, to peace, were disposed;
And I thought making honey might render one sweet
But some here I might find on London's worst street."

"Well, perhaps, not that nasty and, surely, not all
Of the folks hereabout are the type which would gall
And would menace their neighbours – I've long understood,
When it comes right down to it, most people are good."

THE BEES

"Mister Wilkinson-Hugh, your last point, I'd dispute,
For it is, in most cases, the least attribute
That's the one overlooked by the criminal mind -
It's the trifling clue which that mind leaves behind."

"So, tell me what's different, what's subtly changed?
Was somebody's life recently rearranged?
We may not be in search of somebody with bees
And should look at some other than bee devotees."

"You mean it may not have been one of our group?
Well, if that is so, I feel we might recoup
At least some, if not all, of that spirit we'd lost."
Said Wilkinson-Hugh, who'd been counting the cost.

Sherlock thought for a bit but, being new to the game
Of bee-keeping or apiary – *'what's in a name?'* -
He could not offer any direction of thought
In the matter and knew that more facts must be sought.

"Well, we don't have the facts to support that position
And it may well be that someone of ambition
Who's jealous of someone within your alliance
Has acted with malice and outright defiance."

"We must visit the site where the bees were attacked -
We may still find the signs where the hives had been stacked;
Though I fear, on the mess, your group was fixated,
And most clues, in the clean-up, were obliterated."

"That is probably so – we all pitched in that day;
For, to help out another in need, is the way
Of our group and community– that fact's paramount."
Said Wilkinson-Hugh, *"On each other, we count."*

"Twenty hives were destroyed and their contents all spilled
But, before all that happened, the bees had been killed
By some chemical agent sprayed into each hive -
You would not get off lightly if they were alive."

"Of course, twenty hives out of hundreds might sound
Rather small in proportion but many have found
That their hives have been tampered with, some overturned
And many new boxes for hives have been burned."

"An Arsenic spray, we believe, was the cause
Of the bees being killed – it had given us pause
To consider that one of our number committed
This outrage, and no other thought was permitted."

Holmes said he would like to consider each fact
Which he had at that moment – later on he'd contact
Every apiarist who had some damage inflicted
And then have the guilty one duly convicted.

"Just leave it with me, I will give it much thought;
My methods are such that, for some time, I ought
To dig deep in my memory seeking to find
All the facts of a case of a similar kind."

"For the criminal mind, although cunning and sly,
Will not think a crime through and always wonders why
I am able to see that small clue that I need,
For most criminal planning is blinded by greed."

Holmes went back to his room and he took out his pipe
And, with time-honoured ritual, asked it to wipe
Away all of the mist which was clouding his mind -
He'd search through his brain-attic for what he might find.

Holmes sat and he puffed and he pondered at length -
His tobacco held out but was of such a strength
That he found this two-piper reduced down to one -
In one half an hour, he found he was done.

His brain, nicotine-charged, summarised all the facts
Which he knew about all of these destructive acts;
It then asked itself questions, made statements to muse,
Contemplated if this was some intricate ruse.

"Would there be some advantage this late in the season?
Was greed the main factor? Was vengeance the reason
That hives were destroyed? Did someone in the Guild
Have someone to bring down or position to build?"

"The Guild and its members would, much like the bee,
Repair much of the damage and, should they all see
Their attacker nearby, be enraged and emerge,
And with venomous stings, on their foe, all converge."

"These crimes carry risks, for the apiarists would
Be about tending hives and if somebody should
Approach any hives, surely someone would see
And come down on that person like some angry bee."

"Has there been, recently, any great glut of honey
Which would work to reduce someone's inflow of money?
Could wrecking the hives be a way to reduce
Their production and, so, higher prices, induce?"

But, as Sherlock dug deeper, he heard himself say,
"Surely this cannot be Moriarty at play.
He cannot have followed me here to the Downs -
I've retired – I'm not looking to wear any crowns."

Sherlock shook off the thought and he jumped to his feet
And he said to himself, *"There's a challenge to meet
And I can't be concerned with phantoms running 'round
In my head – there's a killer of bees to be found."*

So he questioned the apiarists, all, one by one,
But deduced, by the time the last one had been done,
That no probable suspect stood out from the rest
And all he'd achieved was to clear them, at best.

*"I will ask around town, for some gossip will flow
Through a village community – someone will know
Anyone who's disgruntled, who's been underpaid,
Whose accounts, overdue, have somehow been mislaid."*

*"Has someone bought a horse which had one leg quite lame?
Did somebody cheat in the big poker game?
Did someone run off with another man's wife?
Or is someone resentful of some other's life?"*

Sherlock thought, topping up his tobacco supply,
He should ask the shopkeeper – he's sure to know why
Anyone might hate bees - all those questions, he'd ask,
Because shopkeepers all would be up to that task.

Wallace Jenkins, the shopkeeper, said, *"Well, I never!
Mister Holmes you are right but you're not that clever.
The questions you've asked on the cause of that crime
Would depict the town perfectly much of the time."*

*"But, now that you ask, two years past, perhaps three,
There had been a young woman stung, not by a bee,
But a dozen or more on the side of her face
When some hives had been left far too close to her place."*

"She had quite a reaction and quite nearly died,
But whoever had placed the hives certainly lied
About having done so – all the hives disappeared
And all trace of who owned them was thoroughly cleared."

"Now, what was her name? Ah, yes! Fellows – that's it.
And her brother was angry – enraged, quite a bit
At the time, for he'd told some hive owners to take
Their hives far from his house for his young sister's sake."

"The young woman survived, but she had a few scars
On her face – they were like a collection of stars.
Her brother then threatened to shoot anyone
Placing hives near his home as somebody had done."

"Rod Fellows, that's him – but he's not a bad chap;
He lives just out of town and he rents out a trap
And a few riding horses – does jobs around town -
But, just mention his sister, he give you a frown."

"No one ever sees her; she was set to wed
But, when all of this happened, she took to her bed
And broke off her engagement. The case is quite sad
For I'm told Bess' scarring is not all that bad."

Holmes thanked Mister Jenkins, then set off to find
If this brother called Fellows might be of the kind
To take vengeance upon all the bee-keeping set.
Was he of the type who would never forget?

Finding Fellows at home, Sherlock asked if he might
Seek his help and his knowledge selecting the right
Type of land and equipment he'd need to begin
A apiarian enterprise, this region, herein.

"Mister Holmes, you must know of what happened to Bess
And that I don't like bees - and beekeepers, much less.
So, why are you here? You'll get no help from me.
So I'll ask to leave and to just let us be."

"The Apiarists' Guild has engaged me to find,"
Replied Sherlock, *"whoever it is that's behind*
The destruction of hives and the killing of bees -
I just try to be subtle with interviewees."

"A good word, that – 'subtle' – but bees didn't know
What the word ever meant; now my sister's face shows
The results of my subtlety with all those men."
Said Fellows, quite angry, *"Away with you, then."*

"Do you know that my sister's completely depressed?
Do you know how I felt when, to me, she confessed
That her life has no value – she wished she were dead -
I cannot get the words she spoke out of my head."

"She won't see her fiancé – they were to be wed
Nearly two years ago but the bees' attack led
To some breakdown which made her despise her own face -
Mister Holmes, what they did was an outright disgrace."

"I had asked for the hives near our house to be moved
But no one knew who owned them, but they all approved
Of the hives being left; but, after the attack,
They were moved in an instant and never came back."

"If I knew who had damaged the hives, I'd not tell,
And there isn't a force on this Earth to compel
Me to do so –I'm glad that the bees have been killed
And the fact that it irks all those men leaves me thrilled."

Sherlock rose and said, *"Thank you, I do understand.*
On your time I shall make no more further demand.
I will make my report but some facts I may keep
To myself and consider the keeping of sheep."

The Apiarists' Guild was appraised of each fact
Although Sherlock's report was not fully exact;
He held back that Fellows said he had been thrilled
And was glad of their anguish at bees being killed.

"I believe Fellows guilty – though, prove it, I can't
And to push him much further, I must say, I shan't;
Some remorse for what happened is long overdue -
Gentleman, really, this could be your cue."

"I'd suggest to you all," Sherlock said, *"to decide*
To show mercy to Fellows and take him aside;
Take him into your group – show him how to keep hives -
By such action you'll add so much more to your lives."

"He is liable for damage – no argument there,
But, within your hearts, you might just find, somewhere
To accept that his mind, at the time of his action,
Had been pushed to the point of its utter distraction."

"His sister's bed-ridden for much of the time -
It's not only her face but something quite sublime
In that part of her brain which affords her esteem -
When that's lost, it can be very hard to redeem."

"I feel that, to some extent, limited fault
Lies with someone whose bees made that fateful assault
After it was requested to move them elsewhere -
The sister was scared of the hives being there."

"The fact hives were moved afterwards says, to me,
That somebody felt guilty enough so that he
Wanted no one to know of the part he had played -
I don't know who that was, but I am quite dismayed."

"It is your decision, but so often I've seen
That a man, gone astray, when forgiven has been
A most worthy companion, a comrade with pride,
And a credit to all who have stood by his side."

"I've seen evil aplenty and many foul crimes;
I've seen granted, forgiveness, on quite a few times;
If your foe's now your ally, your victory's doubled -
No longer will you or your bee-hives be troubled."

"If it's left to the Law, there'll be no room to move -
For the Law's only function is, simply, to prove
Someone guilty then order the penalty set -
Then the lawbreaker's marked – the Law will not forget."

"And many's the man who has mended his ways
Then decided to live by the Law all his days;
And I'm sure there are some standing here on this spot
Who've done things in the past they had wished they had not."

"Be resolute, Gentlemen, but also leave room
In your hearts for the flower which has yet to bloom -
For, that new flower blooming, though once indiscreet,
Yields up nectar and honey that's ever so sweet."

Having told the Guild members his thoughts on the matter,
Holmes stepped from the hall while a great deal of chatter
Came forth from the group, then he heard someone say:
"You are right, Mister Holmes, we'll do it your way."

"Capital, Gentlemen! You will never regret
The decision you made, and I'll never forget
What good friends I have made in the very short while
I have been on these Downs." Sherlock said with a smile.

Well, the mystery was solved and revenge was averted
But it seems Sherlock's mind had been clearly diverted
Away from the peace of the Downs he had sought -
In his mind, the desire for the chase had been wrought.

Sherlock Holmes hadn't realised his mind had reset
Itself back to that mode in which crime must be met
With determined resolve by the forces which stood
For good order, as bad must be countered by good.

More than that, being absent, Holmes' presence was missed
By the very same people who'd recently hissed.
While his search for a culprit had been underway,
All the forces of destiny had been in play.

THE TRIUMPH

Just a little by-line, half way down on the right
Of the Down's weekly paper, said Sherlock's insight
Worked to rescue the area's honey production
By putting in play his great powers of deduction.

The news found its way into each London paper:
"Sherlock Holmes is abuzz in the bee killer's caper."
He was not ridiculed as he had been before -
"Sherlock Holmes, we believe, is the bees-knees once more."

"*Such fickleness,*" Holmes, to himself, had to think,
"*Just a few months ago, had brought, up to the brink
Of despair, my emotions which I keep repressed
As a matter of course, and would not have expressed.*"

The Strand even suggested to Watson, he might
Start to put pen to paper so he might delight,
Once again, avid readers with stories of crime
And how Sherlock solved cases with insight sublime.

Perhaps it could offer some extra incentive -
Its readers were found to be most inattentive
To mundane reports from a boring detective
From Scotland Yard's finest – "*His writing's defective.*"

"*Our readers need heroes and want justice done
By a noble defender who really is one
Of their own, and not part of some uniformed set -
One who'll capture the felons who slip through the net.*"

"*But a hero, also, who's the type of a man
Who will use his discretion whenever he can;
He might offer compassion if, promise, he saw,
Or, if evil, would summon the forces of Law.*"

Watson thought it was time he should visit his friend
To see if his great mind, which had started to mend
At the time he departed, was healthy and hale -
He embarked for the Downs in a late-Autumn gale.

It would be a surprise, he would simply appear;
And as luck might have had it, the weather would clear
To reveal the Downs in their bleakest attire -
Watson's wished with his heart for a great roaring fire.

With the land looking bare as the Winter approached,
Holmes found little to do after having been coached
On the business of bees – there was no more to do
But observe what an apiarist must attend to."

The Bee Set was besotted with Fellows, therefore
Holmes had time on his hands, so he thought to explore
Many structures carved into those ripples of chalk,
"What tales might they tell if they only could talk."

He had wandered about throughout most of the day
And, upon his return, gave a heartfelt *"Hooray!"*
At the sight of John Watson - he was quite overcome:
"I have missed you – we made a terrific twosome."

*"We will have a grand dinner of triumph tonight
And ask Wilkinson-Hugh to join us, if he might;
You must tell me what's happened to make you come out
In this weather. Just what is your visit about?"*

Watson said, *"All in good time, My Friend, and you'll hear
My good news which will, no doubt, be a boon to your ear.
But that will have to wait till we're comfortably set
Around a fine table – meanwhile do not fret."*

That evening, the trio dined well and conversed;
Although Watson, of course, was completely immersed
In a lively account of the Strand's proposition,
Fishing, of course, for Sherlock's disposition.

*"As you've time in excess of your needs, I propose
We put both heads together and try to compose
A new series of stories of crimes we have solved
With the stress on your methods which had been involved."*

Holmes listened intently as Watson described
The Strand's generous offer – it was like being bribed;
He wasn't convinced by the mention of fees,
But made no further mention of working with bees.

William Wilkinson-Hugh had stayed silent until
He could see Watson's discourse begin to instil
Renewed interest in Holmes to return to the fight
Against crime in the city – he knew what was right.

"On our Downs, Mister Holmes, you are feeling quite vexed
With the subject of bees and are somewhat perplexed
In your feelings towards settling down at a time
When you know you are in what you might call your Prime."

"Perhaps it's the time to return to your calling -
I'm told that, in London, the crime rate's appalling;
With Police overstretched, London surely needs one
Who can find clever felons and bring them undone."

"As well, as we've learned, it's so often the case
That the person you've caught at the end of a chase
Is not evil by nature and might well repay
Any chance you might give him by finding his way."

"You have shown us, with Fellows, how we might regain
Our respect for each other; we'll never again
Stoop to nasty assumption and running 'round blind,
But act only on facts as you do in your mind."

"How many in London, and elsewhere, perhaps,
Would be out picking pockets or picking up scraps
If you hadn't afforded a legal exemption
To them when they've erred, and the chance of redemption?"

"How many of these might be locked in a cell,
Forced to linger for years, when some mercy might quell
All their wicked desires and give them a chance
To live out a good life and to, even, advance?"

"How many, as well, in whom devils reside
And who are, by their nature, forever outside
The domain of the just, would be now liberated
Instead of being dutifully incarcerated?"

"Your work is inspiring – do not lose the chance
To work hard with your talents and ever enhance
All those lives that you touch in a meaningful way
And, perhaps, prevent others from going astray."

"The bees and the South Downs can wait a few years
Till your usefulness wanes and it simply appears
That your physical strength isn't up to the task
Which a life of detection is surely to ask."

"Then, only then, should you forego the life
Which you currently lead fighting misdeed and strife.
We are given few years to achieve what we may
And it would be a waste to lose one single day."

"You're forever a colleague in our noble band -
You've been voted Life Membership within the Grand
Ancient Guild of Apiarists – you're now one of us -
For our guild it's an honour, for me it's a plus."

Well, forever the pragmatist, Sherlock agreed
That he should leave the Downs and return with all speed
To those dark grimy streets where he's needed the most -
He'd return with his mind exorcised of its ghost.

Watson stood by in silence while Sherlock received
This great honour, and certain Holmes' mind, once deceived
Into seeing arch-felons around every bend,
Had been purged and would never, to such depths, descend.

And so it would seem that, the light, he had seen -
Even Sherlock made fun of the fool he had been
By allowing his fears to distract his great mind -
He was not, he'd insist, the emotional kind.

His powers of deduction were certainly sound
And his good reputation was sure to rebound
By the time he returned – the newspapers now saw
That Sherlock's deductions had nary a flaw.

"*I feel,*" expressed Holmes, "*it was quite premature
To retreat to the South Downs in search of a cure
For the misery which followed my failure to find
Any trace of that felon, that dead mastermind.*"

"*None-the-less, I have managed to put him in chains
In my mind's deepest dungeons, and there he remains;
He may rattle his shackles and bang on the wall
But he'll never come into my thinking at all.*"

"*I've learned much about bees, and their keepers, as well,
And have made many friends whom I'll see when I dwell,
Many years in the future, on England's South Downs
With its mystical landscapes, its magical towns.*"

"*For it will be the case that, at some future date,
To the South Downs, I'll go, and I will dedicate,
To the raising of bees, all the years which remain
Of my life and, from sleuthing, forever refrain.*"

"I may well write a book on the culture of bees,
Looking over a landscape of green grass and trees,
Though I fear that my past will, at times, seek me out
And the call of helpless, I never will flout."

"That's a bridge I must cross when it's come to, My Friend,
There will always be some needy folk to defend
Against evil and villainy, avarice, greed -
I fear, while I live, my skills, some will need."

"But, for now, I must work at the job I do best
For the criminal classes are known not to rest;
The mice have been playing and getting quite fat
And, though he's been away, they will now face the cat."

"His teeth have been sharpened, his talons are keen,
His eyesight's much sharper than it's ever been;
His return to the streets of London is announced -
This cat has returned and they'll know when he's pounced."

"That other stray cat which had wanted to scrap
And had tried to entice all the mice to his trap
Has been cast from the limelight in which he once shone -
Moriarty? Bah, Humbug! He's long dead and gone!"

"The people all know it, the Police, too, agree,
That when Sherlock is home all the criminals flee
Or just cease the commission of crime, for they know
That, when Sherlock's around, it is time to lay low."

And, so, Sherlock the Cat, with his whiskers abristle,
Hopped onto the train as it gave a loud whistle
As if to announce to the wide world of crime:
"Sherlock Holmes has come back – you are now out of time!"

Watson noticed how Holmes, coming into the station
In London, developed renewed inspiration
For walking those streets and for being involved
And getting, what most thought unsolvable, solved."

"Watson," he declared, *"we will not catch a cab,*
For, though London is grimy and grubby and drab,
I must get London air in my lungs to forget
What I've left on the Downs – I've no time to regret."

The illustrious pair sent their bags on ahead -
Sherlock wished to experience London instead
Of retreating to Baker Street's famous address;
"My ego's afire." to himself, he'd confess.

This desire for esteem, he would try to repress
Because, as a detective, he knew that the less
His emotions and feelings were given their head,
The greater his insightful powers, instead.

But a victory march, of a sort, wouldn't hurt
And, as he strode along, he'd sometimes give a curt
Little nod to admirers, a knowing wry smile -
He'd bask in this limelight for just a short while.

At last, Baker Street came in view, and the pair,
After breathing enough of the city's foul air,
Turned the corner and headed for home and some rest -
Sherlock Holmes had been tested – he knew he was best.

"Sherlock, you're back!" declared Watson with pride,
"And I know, for a while, I had cause to deride
Your obsession with someone whose name I won't say.
Your mind is quite rid of that person, today."

"I believe that you're right for I know I was wrong."
Said Sherlock, *"He's gone and I know I belong*
At the head of the queue for my logical thought -
When it comes to detection, my brain will be sought."

With restored reputation, Holmes swaggered a little
Along Baker Street with his formerly brittle
Self-confidence buoyed by the people who cheered
Even though he knew well some had recently jeered.

But this wasn't the time to look backward, he thought;
It was time to look forward – he knew that he ought
To accept that the Public would cheer or complain
At whatever the thoughts which came forth from his brain.

There were *"well-dones"* galore and a lot of back-slapping
From neighbours, as well as some bouts of hand-clapping;
To himself, he said *"Sherlock, you're back in the game!"*
All replenished in ego, devoid of all shame.

Holmes was nearing his quarters with Watson in tow
When he suddenly started to walk rather slow;
Then he paused at the step and, a note, he could see
Had been pinned to the door of Two-twenty-one-B.

"Ha, Ha!" exclaimed Sherlock to Watson, then yelled
"Do you see it - that note on our door! I'm compelled
To insist that you listen to me and accept
That your judgement, at times, is completely inept."

Watson looked at the note - in his tracks, he stopped dead;
What he saw filled his mind with both terror and dread;
He started to shake, his voice failed him badly
As he raved like a fool and he ranted quite madly.

On their door straight ahead in red letters, quite bold,
Was a message to render his blood icy cold;
"My Dear Doctor Watson, when bear hunts you desire,
Is it Holmes you'd profess or Maurie Hardy, Esquire?"

****

Also from MX Publishing

MX Publishing is the world's largest specialist Sherlock Holmes publisher, with over a hundred titles and fifty authors creating the latest in Sherlock Holmes fiction and non-fiction.

From traditional short stories and novels to travel guides and quiz books, MX Publishing cater for all Holmes fans.

The collection includes leading titles such as *Benedict Cumberbatch In Transition* and *The Norwood Author* which won the 2011 Howlett Award (Sherlock Holmes Book of the Year).

MX Publishing also has one of the largest communities of Holmes fans on Facebook with regular contributions from dozens of authors.

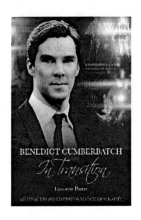

www.mxpublishing.com

Also from MX Publishing

Our bestselling short story collections 'Lost Stories of Sherlock Holmes', 'The Outstanding Mysteries of Sherlock Holmes', 'Untold Adventures of Sherlock Holmes' (and the sequel 'Studies in Legacy') and 'Sherlock Holmes in Pursuit'.

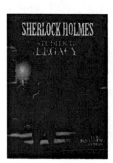

www.mxpublishing.com

Also from MX Publishing

Lego Sherlock Holmes

Six original adventures from Sir Arthur Conan Doyle,
re-illustrated in Lego.

In this book series, the short stories comprising The Adventures of
Sherlock Holmes have been amusingly illustrated using only
Lego® brand minifigures and bricks. The illustrations recreate,
through custom designed Lego models, the composition of the
black and white drawings by Sidney Paget that accompanied the
original publication of these adventures appearing in The Strand
Magazine from July 1891 to June 1892.

www.mxpublishing.com

Also from MX Publishing

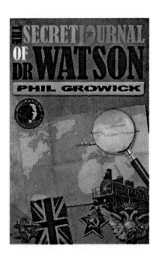

"Phil Growick's, 'The Secret Journal of Dr Watson', is an adventure which takes place in the latter part of Holmes and Watson's lives. They are entrusted by HM Government (although not officially) and the King no less to undertake a rescue mission to save the Romanovs, Russia's Royal family from a grisly end at the hand of the Bolsheviks. There is a wealth of detail in the story but not so much as would detract us from the enjoyment of the story. Espionage, counter-espionage, the ace of spies himself, double-agents, double-crossers...all these flit across the pages in a realistic and exciting way. All the characters are extremely well-drawn and Mr Growick, most importantly, does not falter with a very good ear for Holmesian dialogue indeed. Highly recommended. A five-star effort."
The Baker Street Society

www.mxpublishing.com

Also from MX Publishing

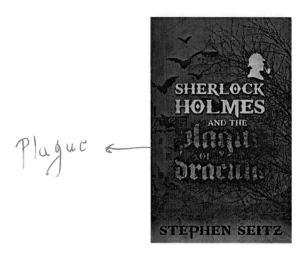

Plague ←

After Mina Murray asks Sherlock Holmes to locate her fiancee, Holmes and Watson travel to a land far eerier than the moors they had known when pursuing the Hound of the Baskervilles. The confrontation with Count Dracula threatens Holmes' health, his sanity, and his life. Will Holmes survive his battle with Count Dracula?

CPSIA information can be obtained
at www.ICGtesting.com
Printed in the USA
LVOW10s2344210318
570756LV00007B/108/P